"Conor, what on earth do you think I am?"

"I think you're a beautiful woman."

"I think you've taken leave of your senses," she retorted, grimly hanging on to her sanity. "Conor, you're not a boy anymore!"

"Would you let me do this if I were?"

"I don't appreciate being put in this position."

"What position?" His thumb brushed her mouth and, almost against her will, her lips parted against that sensuous abrasion.

"How many positions do you know?"

New York Times bestselling author Anne Mather "leaves her legion of fans rejoicing."
—*Romantic Times*

ANNE MATHER began her career by writing the kind of book she likes to read—romance. Married, with two children, this author from the north of England has become a favorite with readers of romance fiction the world over—her books have been translated into many languages and are read in countless countries. Since her first novel was published in 1970, Anne Mather has written more than one hundred romances, with over ninety million copies sold!

Books by Anne Mather

STORMSPELL
WILD CONCERTO
HIDDEN IN THE FLAME
THE LONGEST PLEASURE

HARLEQUIN PRESENTS PLUS
1567—RICH AS SIN
1591—TIDEWATER SEDUCTION

HARLEQUIN PRESENTS
1492—BETRAYED
1514—DIAMOND FIRE
1542—GUILTY
1553—DANGEROUS SANCTUARY

HARLEQUIN ROMANCE
1631—MASQUERADE
1656—AUTUMN OF THE WITCH

ANNE MATHER

Snowfire

Harlequin Books

TORONTO • NEW YORK • LONDON
AMSTERDAM • PARIS • SYDNEY • HAMBURG
STOCKHOLM • ATHENS • TOKYO • MILAN
MADRID • WARSAW • BUDAPEST • AUCKLAND

ISBN 0-373-11617-9

SNOWFIRE

PROLOGUE

HE WAS standing in the dining-room, by the window, gazing out at the rain that had been falling solidly ever since they left the church. Olivia guessed he must be thinking it was an omen. After weeks and weeks of dry weather, it had to be the day of the funeral that it changed.

She halted in the doorway, realising he was not yet aware of her presence, and dreading the moment when she would have to say goodbye. If only she were older, she thought. If only Sally had considered before blithely making Philip her son's guardian. But who would have expected Sally and Keith to die before either of them was thirty-five? And Philip was Sally's brother. He was obviously the natural choice.

Even so...

Olivia caught her lower lip between her teeth as she stared at the boy's drooping figure. Today had been more of a strain for him than for anyone, and his bent head and hunched shoulders spoke of a misery he could no longer hide. He had done well, she thought, handling himself through the tortuous rites of the burial with a dignity and self-possession enviable in a much older man. But now, believing himself unobserved, he had given way to his real feelings, and Olivia's heart went out to him as she recognised his grief.

'Conor.'

His name was barely audible across the silent room, but he heard her. He turned then, dashing his hand over his face as he did so, struggling to resume the defensive posture that had kept his tears at bay.

'Oh—hi, Aunt 'Livia,' he said, forcing a smile that was determinedly bright. 'I was just watching the rain.

The garden's waterlogged. Mum's——' He broke off
abruptly as the mention of his mother's name discon-
certed him, and then continued with an obvious effort,
'Mum's dahlias are really taking a hammering.'

'Are they?'

Olivia came to stand beside him, noticing almost in-
consequentially that he had grown another couple of
inches in the last twelve months. He was almost as tall
as she was now, and at five feet seven inches—nine in
her heels—she was considered above average height.

But now she feigned an interest in the flowers Sally
had planted in the borders. The rain-soaked garden
showed little of the colour it had flaunted earlier in the
summer. The last time Olivia was here they had all had
tea on the lawn...

She glanced at the boy beside her, more concerned
about him than about his mother's flowers. What was
he really thinking? she wondered. Was he wishing he
had gone with his parents on that fated day trip to Paris?
He looked so pale and drawn, his sandy hair, which
always seemed to need cutting, straggling over the collar
of his dark suit.

If only they had made her his guardian, she thought
helplessly. At fifteen, a boy needed to know who he was;
he needed roots. Everything he knew and loved was here
in Paget. He knew no one in the United States. He hadn't
even been to Florida for a holiday.

'Do I have to go?'

The low, impassioned words were uncannily like an
echo of her own thoughts, and Olivia wondered if he
could read her mind. Certainly her association with the
Brennans had always been a close one, and only in the
last couple of years, since she had gone to live and work
in London, had their friendship suffered because of the
separation.

Of course, it was his mother with whom Olivia had
had the most in common, she acknowledged. She had
been ten when Keith and Sally Brennan had moved into

the big old house next to her grandmother's cottage.
And, from the beginning, she had been a welcome visitor
there. Naturally the fact that the Brennans had also had
a baby son had been a great attraction, but as Olivia
grew older it was Sally who had shared all the hopes and
fears of her teenage years.

Olivia had hardly known her own parents. They had
been involved in a car accident when she was little more
than a baby herself, and although her mother had
lingered on in the hospital for several weeks after the
crash there had never been any real hope of her recovering consciousness. In consequence, Olivia's paternal
grandmother had taken her to live with her and, although
Mrs Holland had done her best, she had been too used
to living alone to have much patience with a lively
toddler.

That was why Olivia felt such an enormous sense of
empathy with Conor now. She had known him since he
was two years old. She had watched him grow from a
mischievous schoolboy into a confident teenager. She had
combed his hair and scrubbed his knees, and sometimes
told him off. And lately she had teased him about his
girlfriends: the procession of budding Madonnas who
hung around outside his gate. He was the closest thing
to a nephew she was ever likely to have, and she was
going to miss him badly.

'I—think so,' she answered now, finding it difficult
to say the words with his anxious eyes upon her. She
struggled to sound optimistic. 'Look at it this way—it'll
be a fresh start. And—where your Uncle Philip lives
sounds really beautiful. Imagine being able to swim all
the year round!'

'I don't want to go.' Conor's response was desperate.
'I want to stay here. Why can't I stay here? This house
is mine now, isn't it?'

'Well, yes, but——'

'There you are, then.'

'Conor, you can't stay here alone!' It wasn't as if her grandmother still lived next door. Last year Mrs Holland had had a stroke, and she had been moved into a retirement home. The cottage had been sold, and Sally had said they hardly knew the new occupants.

'Why can't I?' he demanded now. 'I've stayed here on my own before.'

'Not for weeks you haven't,' replied Olivia flatly, finding it impossible to sustain his cornered gaze. 'Conor, you're only fifteen——'

'Sixteen,' he interrupted her swiftly. 'I'll be sixteen in three months.'

'No, Conor.'

'Then why can't I come and live with you?' he demanded, seizing on the idea. 'I wouldn't get in your way, honestly. I could get a job——'

'Conor…' She sighed. 'Conor, you have to finish your education. It's what your parents would have wanted.'

'In Florida!' His lips twisted.

'Yes.' Olivia knew she had to be firm.

Conor sniffed. 'I see.'

'Oh, don't say it like that.' She couldn't bear his defeated stare. 'If there was anything I could do——'

'—you'd do it. I know.' But Conor sounded horribly cynical. 'I'm sorry. I should have realised. You're going to be a hotshot lady lawyer! The last thing you need is a raw kid hanging around your apartment, cramping your style, when you bring clients home——'

'Conor, I don't have an apartment, and you know it,' she protested weakly. 'I have a room in a house that I share with three other women. It's just a bed-sit, really. And there's no way you could live there.'

'Well, why can't you get something bigger? Something we could share? I'd help with the rent——'

'No, Conor.' Olivia squashed that idea once and for all. 'I'm not your guardian,' she explained gently. 'Your Uncle Philip is. Even . . . even if it were possible—which

it's not,' she put in hurriedly, 'he wouldn't allow you to
stay with me.'

'And aren't you glad?' Conor's expression changed
to one of bitterness. He swung away from her, thrusting
aggressive hands into his trouser pockets, rounding his
shoulders against an unforgiving fate. 'I bet you can't
wait to get in your car and drive away from all this, can
you?' he exclaimed scornfully. 'It's not your problem,
so why get involved? I don't know what you came here
for. You can't help, so why didn't you stay away?'

'Oh, Conor!'

Olivia's composure broke at last, and, as if her grief
was all that was needed to drive a wedge through his
crumbling defiance, he turned back to her. For a few
tense moments he just stared at her, and she saw the
glitter of tears on lashes several shades darker than his
hair. Then, with a muffled groan, he flung himself into
her arms.

He was shaking. She could feel it. And his thin, boyish
frame seemed even bonier than she remembered. One
of the neighbours had told her he hadn't eaten a thing
since he had learned that the plane carrying his mother
and father to Paris had exploded over the Channel. He
had borne it all bravely, but inside it was eating him up.

'I'm sorry, I'm sorry,' he muttered at last, dragging
himself away from her. He rubbed the back of his hand
across his cheek, looking at her rather shamefacedly.
'I've wet the collar of your blouse.'

'It doesn't matter.' Olivia wished the dampness she
could feel against her neck was all she had to worry
about. 'I just wish there was something I could do. Your
mother was my best friend. I don't want to let you down.'

Conor's lashes drooped to veil eyes that were presently a watery shade of green. He had long lashes for a
boy, and they did a successful job of hiding his feelings.
Dear God, why had this had to happen? The Brennans
had been such a close family. They had come to live in
Paget when Keith, who was a physiotherapist, got an

appointment at the hospital in nearby Dymchurch. Sally, meanwhile, had been content doing social work and looking after her garden, and Conor had been the centre of their universe...

'What time are you leaving?' he enquired abruptly, and she guessed what it must have cost him to ask that question. But he knew, as well as she did, that it would take her some time to drive back to London. And now that the nights were drawing in again...

'Um—pretty soon,' Olivia answered now, putting out her hand to brush a thread of lint from his jacket, and then withdrawing it again as he flinched away from her touch. She linked her hands together instead in an effort to control her own anguish, and glanced behind her. 'I— you will write and let me know your address, won't you? You know where I live, and I'm looking forward to hearing all about Port Douglas.'

Conor shrugged. 'If you like.'

There was a flatness to his tone now, an indifference, and inwardly Olivia groaned. It was foolish, she knew, but the thought of leaving him, of not seeing him again for God knew how long, was tearing her apart, and she realised she had to get away before she gave in and said something she would regret. He couldn't stay with her. There was no way she could support herself *and* a boy of his age. And it was no use toying with the idea of abandoning her legal training, getting a job down here, and offering to live with him, in this house, as a kind of guardian-cum-housekeeper. Philip Cox would never allow it. And, in any case, the house was probably going to be sold to pay for Conor's education.

Biting her lip, she took a steadying breath. 'So,' she said, striving for control, 'you're going to be all right?'

Conor's mouth twisted. 'Of course.'

Olivia hesitated. 'You do—understand?'

Conor shrugged. 'Does it matter?'

'Of course it matters.' Just for a moment Olivia lost her hard-won detachment, and a little of her own frustration showed in her voice. 'I want you to be happy, Conor. And you will be. Believe me!'

CHAPTER ONE

THE small hotel, part of a row of wood-faced Tudor-type dwellings, many of which owed their origins to the days when the Cinque Ports provided ships to fight the Spanish Armada, stood at the end of the quay. Of course, the old buildings had been much renovated and repaired since Elizabethan times, but the Ship Inn's low doorways and timbered ceilings were too attractive to tourists to be replaced, however inconvenient they might be.

Not that Paget attracted as many visitors as Romney, or Hythe, or Dymchurch. It was too small, for one thing, and, for another, the salt-marshes were not suitable for children to play on. But, as a fishing village that hadn't altered drastically since the sixteenth century, it was one of a kind, and many visitors, Americans particularly, came to take photographs of its ancient buildings and cobbled streets.

But at this time of the year there were few tourists stalwart enough to brave the east wind that came in over the marshes. The first weeks of February had been wild and blustery, and only that morning there had been a sprinkling of snow over the fishing boats lying idle in their stocks. Storm warnings had been out all along the coast, and the few fishermen willing to venture out into the choppy waters had been driven back again by the gales.

Standing at her bedroom window, her head stooped to accommodate the low lintel, Olivia felt no sense of regret at the inclement weather. On the contrary, it suited her very well that she did not have to put on a sociable face when she went down to the tiny dining-room for breakfast. She hadn't come to Paget for familiarity or company. She didn't want to talk to anybody, beyond

12

the common courtesies politeness demanded. Because he hadn't recognised her name, the landlord had assumed she was a stranger here, and it had suited her to foster that belief. As far as Tom Drake was concerned, she was one of 'them crazy Londoners', she was sure. Who else would choose to come to Paget while winter still gripped it in its icy grasp? Who else would book a room for an unspecified period when it was obvious from her appearance that she would have benefited from a spell in the sun?

Of course, the fact that she looked thin and pale and tended to drag her left leg might have given the staff other ideas, Olivia acknowledged. After all, this was hardly the sort of place to come for a rest cure. Perhaps they thought she had some awful terminal illness and had come to Paget to die. It was impossible to speculate what they might think, but in the week that had elapsed since she came here they had respected her privacy and left her alone.

And Olivia was grateful. In fact, for the first time in more than a year she actually felt as if she was beginning to relax. Her leg was still painful, particularly if she walked further than the doctors had recommended. But her appetite was improving a little, and she didn't always need barbiturates to sleep.

Her lips curled slightly as she accorded that thread of optimism the contempt it deserved. Imagine needing drugs to enjoy a night's rest, she thought bitterly. She was thirty-four, and she felt at least twenty years older!

But her low state of fitness was not entirely unwarranted, she defended herself. The shock of learning that Stephen had been unfaithful had barely been blunted when the accident happened, and weeks spent in a hospital bed had served to exacerbate her sense of betrayal. If she'd been able to carry on with her work, lose herself in its legal intricacies, she might have weathered the storm fairly well. It wasn't as if her marriage to Stephen had been ideal from the outset. It hadn't, and it had taken her only a short time to acknowledge that she had allowed her biological clock to induce her into a situation that was primarily the result of pressure. Pressure from her friends, pressure from her peers, but also pressure within herself at the knowledge that she was twenty-nine, single, and facing a lonely future. In consequence, she had allowed herself to be persuaded that any marriage was better than no marriage at all, and it wasn't until the deed was done that she had realised how wrong she was.

She couldn't altogether blame Stephen. Like herself, he had been approaching an early middle age without a permanent companion, and, if some of his habits had been a little annoying, and his lovemaking less than earth-moving, she had determined to make the best of it. No doubt there were things she did that annoyed him, too, and if her grandmother had taught her anything, it was that life was seldom the way one wanted it to be.

But, predictably enough, she supposed, it was Stephen who tired of the marriage first. And, equally predictably, she was the last to find out. Perhaps if her job had not been so demanding, if she had not spent so many evenings visiting clients or preparing briefs, she would have noticed sooner what was going on. But Stephen's job in wholesaling meant that he was often away overnight, and it wasn't until a well-meaning friend had asked if she had enjoyed her mid-week break in Bath that she had been curious enough to examine their credit-card statements more closely. What she had found was that Stephen often occupied a double room on his nights away, and that, while this was not so incriminating in itself, another receipt, showing dinner for two at a bistro in Brighton, was. Olivia knew that Stephen had purportedly gone to Brighton to attend a delegates' conference, and the presentation dinner that followed it had supposedly been a dead bore.

When she confronted him with her suspicions, he had tried to deny it. For all the inadequacies of their marriage, he had still wanted to maintain the status quo. It had suited him to have a wife who wouldn't divorce him hovering in the background. It gave him an excuse not to get too involved, and he'd enjoyed the thrill of forbidden fruit.

For Olivia, however, the idea of continuing such an alliance was abhorrent to her. She wanted out. She had learned her lesson, and she wanted her freedom, and Stephen's pleas to give him another chance only filled her with disgust.

Nevertheless, although she moved out of the apartment they had shared in Kensington, Stephen had continued to hound her. Even though she employed a solicitor in another partnership to represent her, Stephen insisted he would fight the petition in court. And Olivia knew, better than anyone, how messy such divorces could be. And how ironic that she should be caught in such a situation which could only be damaging to her career.

In the years since she had become an articled solicitor she had gained a small reputation for competent representation. She still worked for the large partnership with whom she had trained, but her obvious abilities had not gone unnoticed. There was talk of a junior partnership, if she wanted it, or the possibility of branching out on her own. Neither option would benefit from adverse publicity of any kind, and Olivia knew Stephen would do anything to embarrass her. He was bitter and resentful, and, incredibly, he blamed her for their estrangement. He was not going to let her go easily, and his threats were a constant headache.

Which was probably why the accident had happened, she acknowledged now, even though she had never blamed Stephen for any of it. She had already been sleeping badly, and the extra hours at work she had been putting in, in an effort to keep other thoughts at bay, had taken their toll. She shouldn't have been driving. She should have taken a taxi to the station, and caught a train to Basingstoke. But she hadn't. She had driven—

straight into one of the concrete pillars supporting a bridge over the M3. Or at least, that was what they had told her. She didn't remember anything after leaving the office.

Of course, Stephen had been sorry then. He had come to see her in the hospital, when she was still strung up to so many machines that she must have looked like a marionette. She could have her divorce now, he'd said. He wouldn't oppose it. He'd contact her solicitor straight away, and get the thing in motion. It wasn't until later that she'd wondered at his speed.

By then, by the time she was lucid enough to understand that she was lucky to be alive, she had had other problems to contend with. Not least the news that, although her skull was evidently thicker than it had a right to be, and her wounds would heal, and her broken limbs would mend, her left leg had suffered multiple fractures, and it was unlikely she would ever run again.

She remembered she'd tried to joke about not being able to run before, but, as time went on, she realised what they had been trying to tell her. Her left leg had been crushed, badly crushed, and, although all the skills of modern surgery had been brought to bear, the tendons had been damaged quite beyond repair.

Physiotherapy had helped a lot. That and her determination to walk again. When she first left the hospital she had had to get around on crutches, and for weeks she had struggled to and from the clinic in an ambulance. But gradually she had been able to put the crutches aside and manage with a walking-stick, even taking up her job again, although that had been rather harder. Her leg ached if she had to stand for any length of time, and the stress of both the accident and the divorce had taken a toll on her defences. Eventually, she had had to accept that if she wasn't careful she was going to have a complete nervous breakdown, and the senior partner at Hallidays had suggested she take a holiday.

Olivia knew he had had something different in mind from the east coast of southern England. The West Indies, perhaps, or South America. Somewhere where the sun was hot and life was lived at a slower pace. Somewhere she could relax, and restore the tattered remnants of her existence.

Of course, her colleagues didn't know the whole story. They had assumed that Stephen's defection had precipitated this crisis. But the truth was that the weeks of inactivity had given Olivia time to re-evaluate her life, and, despite a sense of frustration at her weakness, she was no longer sure of what she wanted.

For so long her career had been the yardstick by which she had measured her success. She had wanted to become a lawyer, and she had succeeded. She had wanted to be offered a partnership, and that, too, was within her grasp. So why did it all seem so empty, somehow? What had happened to the ambition that had sustained her for so long?

She had tried to tell herself that it was the old biological thing again. That, however pointless her marriage to Stephen had become, it had still been her best chance to fulfil herself as a woman. If she had had a baby, would things have been different? They had never taken any precautions, but it had evidently been not to be. Maybe she couldn't have children. Maybe that was why she felt so empty now. Or was it, as Conor had said once, that she had got hard in her old age? But then, he had wanted to hurt her, and undoubtedly he had succeeded.

Conor...

Leaving the window, Olivia crossed to the dressing-table and seated herself on the padded stool in front of the mirror. As she examined her pale features without pleasure, she wondered where he was, and what he was doing now. It must be—what?—nine years since she'd seen him. In fact she had only seen him that one time since he had gone to live in the United States.

She grimaced. It was not a visit she remembered with any affection. At seventeen and a half, Conor had changed totally from the sensitive boy she had known. He had been loud, and cocky, and objectionable, full of his own importance and brimming with conceit. He had been in London with a group of students from the college he attended in Port Douglas, and he had arrived at the house she still shared one night, already the worse for drink.

To Olivia, who was used to the Conor she knew from the letters he had occasionally sent her, he was almost a stranger, bragging about the life he led back in Florida, impressing her with the parties he went to, the car he drove. He was arrogant and brash, decrying the room she had furnished with such care, and disparaging her lifestyle compared to his. He had said she was a fool to spend all her time working, that he was glad he'd got out of England when he had. And when Olivia had defended herself by taking a stiff-necked stance, he had accused her of getting hard in her old age.

Oh, yes. Olivia traced the curve of one eyebrow with a rueful finger. That visit had not been repeated. Indeed, it had taken her quite some time to get over it, and when there were no more letters she wasn't really surprised. Who'd have thought it? she mused. That two years should have made such a difference. But then, he *had* been young, she conceded, as she had done numerous times before. Perhaps it had been his way of dealing with the situation. There was no doubt that losing both his parents had been quite a blow.

Still, in spite of the lapse in communication, she did continue to think about him sometimes. Particularly times like this, when she was feeling rather low. Which was probably why she had chosen to come to Paget, even though, since her grandmother's death five years ago, she had no connection with the place. She hadn't wanted to go anywhere hot and noisy. She supposed what she'd really wanted to do was return to her roots.

A final grimace at her appearance, and she was ready to go downstairs. The trouble with very dark hair, particularly the unruly variety, was that it accentuated any trace of pallor in her face, she thought ruefully. Since the accident it had grown so long that she was obliged to confine it in a knot at her nape, and even then it contrived to escape every hairpin. She looked like a witch, she decided, all wild hair and black-ringed eyes. It was a reminder—if any reminder was needed—of why she had always kept her hair short in the past.

She left the walking-stick propped by the door. Slowly but surely, she was managing to do without it for a little longer every day. Eventually, she told herself, only the slight dragging of her foot and the ugly scars that would never completely disappear would be all that remained of her trauma. And in three weeks she'd possess her decree absolute, and Stephen would no longer play any part in her future.

Poor Stephen, she thought, with an unwarranted sense of pity. He hadn't been able to wait to dissociate himself from any responsibility for what had happened to her. He had got quite a shock when he saw her in the hospital. He must have been afraid he was going to be tethered to an invalid for the rest of his life.

Men! She shook her head regretfully as she closed her door behind her. Her experience of the opposite sex was that a woman should not rely on them. Olivia determined that, whatever she decided to do, she would not be taken in again. She was free—or she would be in three weeks—over twenty-one, and independent. What did she need a man for?

Since she was the only guest staying at the inn right now, Mrs Drake always made a fuss of her after she'd negotiated the narrow, twisting stairs that led down to the lower floor. Seating her at the much-coveted table in the leaded window embrasure, the publican's plump wife rattled through a series of questions about how she was, whether she'd slept well, had she everything she needed, and, finally, what did she fancy for breakfast this morning?

As she only ever had coffee and toast, that question was really academic, but, as always, Olivia answered her, adding a polite enquiry as to her and Mr Drake's health.

'Oh, we're in the pink, as they say, Mrs Perry,' Mrs Drake assured her, as she usually did. 'But it's a raw morning, that it is. Tom thinks we'll have more snow before nightfall.'

'Do you think so?' Olivia glanced out at the chilly scene beyond the windows. There were few people about, and those who were had their collars up against the wind as they hurried along the flagged quayside.

'So he says,' agreed Mrs Drake, raising her pencilled eyebrows. 'Now, you're sure you wouldn't like a bit of bacon and an egg? A bit of dry toast doesn't seem to have much sustenance in it. Not at this time of the year.'

Her speculative gaze swept critically over her guest's slim figure, and, in spite of the bulkiness of her sweater, Olivia knew she had been assessed and found wanting. Mrs Drake wouldn't say so, of course. Olivia's attitude had not encouraged familiarity. Nevertheless, she was aware that they were curious about her. But for once her disability had provided a useful barrier.

'Just toast, please,' she insisted now, accompanying her refusal with a smile. And Mrs Drake stifled her opposition, taking her dismissal with good heart.

The daily newspaper Olivia had reluctantly ordered when she checked in was lying beside her plate, and although she wasn't much concerned with the politics that had made the headlines she felt obliged to pick it up. There was no television in her room here, even though Mr Drake had said he could arrange for one if she wanted it, and, despite the fact that she had politely declined his offer, it did seem rather childish to cut herself off completely.

She flicked idly through the inner pages, scanning the gossip columns with assumed interest. But the activities of the latest hot property in the pop world seemed aimless, and her eyes drifted back to the Drakes' cat, washing its paws on a pile of nets across the way.

A man strode past the window, hands thrust into the pockets of a leather jacket, his collar tipped against the weather. He was a fairly tall man, solidly, though not stockily built, with fairish hair and skin that was browner that it should have been in this chilly part of the world.

The landlord emerged from the inn as he was walking past, and the two exchanged the time of day. It was a brief encounter, not least because Tom Drake was in his shirt-sleeves, and Olivia guessed the state of the weather had been mentioned. But, as the man lifted a hand to rake back his sandy hair before continuing on his way, she was struck by his resemblance to Conor Brennan. It was a fleeting glimpse, of course, and she guessed there must be dozens of men around who might be said to resemble the youth she remembered. Even so, it was an amazing coincidence, coming as it had on the heels of the thoughts she had had earlier.

Which was probably why she had imagined the resemblance, she conceded to herself now, as Mrs Drake returned with her toast and coffee. She was tempted to ask the woman who Mr Drake had been speaking to, but to do that would invite exactly the kind of questions she was hoping to avoid. It would mean admitting some connection with the village, for why else would she be interested in one of its inhabitants unless there was some reason why she might know him?

In any case, she didn't know the man. It had just been a momentary aberration. If Conor had come back to this country for any reason, surely he would at least have tried to get in touch with her? He might not have her address, but he still knew where she worked.

Her appetite had been negligible since the accident, and this morning was no exception. But the pot of coffee was very welcome, and she managed to swallow half a slice of toast. Then, leaving the warm fire that was

burning in the dining-room, she went back up to her
room. She had decided to go for a walk. So long as she
wrapped up warmly, she would enjoy the exercise.

But today she didn't walk around the harbour and out
on to the breakwater as she usually did. Nor did she
venture across the salt marshes, which, even in winter,
provided a veritable haven for birds. Instead, she decided to test her leg by walking inland, up Paget's cobbled
streets to where houses clustered on the hillside. It was
further than she had ventured before, but it was time
she took a look at her grandmother's old cottage, she
told herself. She refused to admit what her real intentions were. But anyway, what was wrong with being
curious about who was living in the Brennans' house
these days? she argued. It was years since it had been
sold to pay for Conor's education.

Her thigh was aching by the time she reached Gull
Rise. And the irregular row of Victorian dwellings looked
much the same as she remembered them. They were
mostly cottages—some terraced, like her grandmother's, and others independently spaced. The house
the Brennans used to occupy was bigger than the rest,
but Olivia remembered Sally saying they had got it fairly
cheaply, because it had needed so much doing to it. The
young couple had spent their first few years at Gull Rise
renovating the place, and by the time Conor was in his
teens it was a home to be proud of.

It still was, Olivia saw poignantly, her eyes flickering
over her old home and settling on the house next door.
She felt an unfamiliar ache in her throat. Someone had
cared enough about it to keep the exterior bright and
shining, she noticed. The woodwork was newly painted,
and the drive was clear of weeds.

She halted a few yards from the house, on the opposite side of the road. With the collar of her cashmere
coat pulled high about her ears, and her gloved hand
shielding her face, she didn't think anyone would recognise her. Besides, most of her grandmother's old

neighbours had either died or moved away, and the gauntness of her own features would deceive any but her closest friends.

There was a car parked in the drive, she saw — a small Peugeot, with current licence plates. And, even as she watched, a young woman came out of the house and unlocked the car, before pausing, as if someone had attracted her attention. Her blonde head tipped expectantly towards the door of the house, which she had left ajar, and, leaving her keys in the car, she sauntered back.

Her actions spurred Olivia to life. For heaven's sake, she chivvied herself irritably, was she reduced to spying on other people for entertainment? The house was lived in, and evidently by someone who cared. She had satisfied her curiosity, and that was all she needed to know.

But, as she turned away, a man appeared in the doorway across the street. A tall man, with light hair, wearing a black leather jacket. Seen face on, his resemblance to Conor was even more striking, and with a sense of alarm she realised it was him.

But, it couldn't be, her brain insisted, refusing to accept the evidence of her eyes. Conor didn't live in England, he lived in America. There was no way he could have bought this house and settled down here. It was too much of a coincidence. Too incredible to be true.

And yet she lingered, aware that her injured leg was cramping beneath her. Dear God, how was she going to find the strength to walk back to the harbour? she fretted. If she didn't move soon, she was going to collapse on the spot.

But the truth was that the sense of panic she was feeling was as much psychological as physical. Whoever the man was—and the young woman was kissing him now, running a possessive hand down his cheek, and saying something that brought a grin to his lean face—he wouldn't appreciate the thought that she had been prying into his affairs. If it was Conor, he evidently had no need of her assistance.

But it hurt that he should come back to England without even letting her know. She had been his surrogate aunt, for heaven's sake. His parents had been her close friends. And she had known Conor since he was two years old! That should have meant something to the boy he had been.

Of course, he wasn't a boy any more, she acknowledged ruefully. He was a man, and an extremely attractive one at that. Even from a distance, she could see he looked bigger and stronger than his father had ever been. And the young woman, with her silky blonde hair and long, unscarred legs, evidently thought so, too.

Olivia's lips tightened. Who was she? Who were *they*? If it was Conor, was this his wife? And why should it mean so much to her? He obviously didn't desire her approval.

Sucking in her breath as a sharp, stabbing pain shot up her thigh, she made a determined effort to extinguish her curiosity. It was nothing to do with her, she told herself grimly, endeavouring to put one foot in front of the other. She could look in the phone book when she got back to the inn. In fact, she wished she had just done that in the first place. Then she could have made up her mind to ring, or not to ring, without any knowledge of his status.

Tears sprang to her eyes as the wind swept a sudden gust of sleet into her face. Oh, great, she thought bitterly, as the frozen flakes stung her cheeks. This was all she needed: soaking to the skin!

Afterwards, she was never sure how it happened—whether her leg had simply given out on her, or her foot had slipped on a thread of ice. But, whatever the cause, she found herself falling, hitting the pavement heavily, and scraping her gloved palms.

It was so humiliating. She had never considered herself a particularly graceful creature, but she had never been as clumsy as she was now. Landing on her bottom, she

felt a jarring sensation all up her spine, but she knew
she should be grateful she hadn't fallen on her leg.

Blinking back the hot tears that never seemed far away
these days, she was making an ungainly effort to get to
her feet when strong hands gripped her arms. 'Steady,'
said a husky male voice, holding her where she was
without much effort. 'Take it easy, ma'am. You've had
quite a shock.'

HE WAS beside her, not yet able to see her face, and Olivia wished the ground would just open up and swallow her. If she had had any doubts about his identity before, the soft southern drawl had dispelled them. There couldn't be another man who looked like Conor in Paget, not with the same transatlantic accent.

'I'm—fine,' she muttered shortly, shaking off his hands, and keeping her face averted. She was aware that the other woman had come to join them. She had heard the hurried tap of her heels, with the impatient, 'Is she all right?' enquiry, which put Olivia squarely into the category of being a nuisance.

'She says she is,' replied Conor, ignoring the young woman's tone and squatting down on his heels. Even though she couldn't see them, Olivia was aware of his eyes appraising her bent head. 'Are you?'

Olivia sighed. And, with a sense of resignation, she accepted there was no way she was going to be able to avoid the inevitable. Much against her better judgement, she lifted her head, and Conor sucked in his breath with an audible gulp.

'Aunt 'Livia!' he exclaimed, and Olivia thought how typical it was that he should make her feel even older than she did already.

'Hello, Conor,' she responded, taking advantage of his stunned expression to clamber stiffly to her feet. Using the fence of a nearby garden for support, she endeavoured to hide the throbbing pain in her femur, and was inordinately glad she was wearing trousers to hide her leg's wasted appearance. 'I didn't know you were back in England.'

'No.'

Conor seemed to be having some difficulty in adjusting to her appearance, and Olivia lifted a nervous hand to her hair, wondering if she looked as distraught as she felt. It had obviously been a shock for him, seeing her like this, and she guessed he was dismayed at how she'd aged.

'Conor...' The young woman touched his arm as he got dazedly to his feet, and he looked at her almost without recognition. 'Conor,' she said again, 'I didn't know you had relatives in England. Is this your mother's sister or something?'

'No!' The denial he made was vehement, and she widened her big blue eyes in faint alarm.

'But you called——'

'—her Aunt 'Livia. I know,' agreed Conor shortly. He looked at Olivia as if he still couldn't believe his eyes, and then added, half impatiently, 'It was a token form of address, that's all.'

'Then, who is——?'

'I lived next door to Conor and his parents, many years ago,' said Olivia stiffly, glancing down at her coat, and noticing that it had suffered somewhat from the impact. Much like herself, she thought frustratedly. She tested her weight on her injured leg and drew back instantly. Oh, God, it wasn't going to stand her walking on it.

'Oh, I see.' The girl was evidently losing interest in the affair. She jogged Conor's arm, and gestured back across the street. 'Con, I've really got to be going. I told Marie I'd be in at eleven.'

Conor dragged his thoughts back to the present with obvious difficulty. 'Then go,' he said, the indifference in his voice audible to anyone's ears. The relief Olivia had felt when he had been obliged to look away from her was tempered by his evident irritation, and the younger woman's lips tightened with resentment.

'Well, aren't you coming?' she exclaimed. 'I thought you had an appointment at the clinic.'

'I do.' Conor's expression hardened, and for a moment Olivia was reminded of the boy he had once been. But then her brain made the connection between the girl's words and his response, and she wondered with sudden concern why he should be attending a clinic.

The young woman looked at Olivia without liking. 'Aren't you going to introduce us first?' she protested, and Olivia knew that wasn't what she wanted at all. It was just another attempt to extricate Conor from the situation, without leaving him alone with her. Though why she should feel the need to do so, Olivia couldn't imagine.

If only she could leave, she thought. If only she could make some casual excuse for being there, and saunter off along Gull Rise. But every minute she delayed accentuated her growing weakness. She was going to have to get a taxi. Even if it meant knocking on a stranger's door.

'Sharon Holmes; Olivia—Perry,' Conor said now, after a moment's hesitation, and it took a second for Olivia to register that he had used her married name. But before she could wonder how he had found out that she had been married, he had bent, and was running exploring hands over her injured leg.

'Don't do that!' Olivia's horrified objection almost drowned out Sharon's angry, '*Con*!' Both women reacted unfavourably to his outrageous interference, and Olivia shuddered visibly when his hands massaged her calf.

Conor straightened without haste. 'You were standing there like a stork,' he said, his eyes going directly to Olivia's wavering gaze. 'I thought you must have hurt your leg when you fell, but it's more than that, isn't it? I guess you'd better come inside while I make a proper examination.'

Olivia gasped. 'I beg your pardon?'

'I said——'

'I heard what you said,' she retorted, wrapping the folds of the mud-stained cashmere coat closer about her slim figure. 'But I don't want you to give me an examination. You—can call me a taxi, if you like. I admit I don't think I'm up to walking back to my hotel. But that's all, thank you. Just a cab.'

Conor glanced at Sharon, who was staring at him with undisguised irritation, but he chose not to obey the warning in her gaze. 'I'll give you a lift back to where you're staying after you've told me what happened,' he retorted briefly. 'Now, can you walk across to the house or shall I carry you?'

Olivia wished she could tell him what to do with his assistance, but she couldn't. The truth was that she felt as if she were rooted to the spot. The very idea of putting any weight at all on her injured leg was anathema to her. If only she had brought her walking-stick, instead of pretending she didn't need it.

'Like that, is it?'

Conor had evidently read her uncertainty correctly, and, without giving her the opportunity to voice any further protest, he bent and plucked her off the pavement. Then, with the girl, Sharon, fluttering ineffectually at his side, he strode purposefully across the road.

Argument was useless, Olivia decided helplessly, as the welcome relief of being off her feet entirely brought more tears to her eyes. Even the hard strength of his arm beneath her knee was preferable to the agony of continually supporting herself on one leg. He must be strong, she thought, to carry her so effortlessly. He had picked her up as if she were a doll, and he wasn't even breaking sweat.

'Con, what are you going to do?'

Sharon overtook him as he started up the drive, taking little backward running steps in an effort to attract his attention. Olivia, obliged to rest her arm around Conor's neck for support, felt embarrassed at being the cause of her frustration. But what could she do, except promise herself to keep out of their way in future?

'I'm going to give Liv a drink, and then I'm going to take her back to her hotel,' he replied shortly, waiting for her to step aside so that he could mount the steps to the door. 'I thought you were going to work,' he added, as she followed them into the house. 'A few moments ago you were desperate to be gone.'

A few minutes ago she hadn't expected her husband to bring a strange woman into the house, reflected Olivia drily, knowing exactly how Sharon was feeling. But for her to try and excuse herself would bestow the situation with an intimacy it didn't deserve. Besides, Conor had called her *Aunt* 'Livia when he first saw her. Surely Sharon could see she had no competition here?

'Well, are you going to the clinic?'

Sharon's voice had taken on a resentful note now, and this time Olivia felt she had to say something.

'The clinic?' she echoed, as Conor lowered her onto a sofa in the comfortable drawing-room. 'Um—if you have an appointment, oughtn't you to keep it? I mean, if you need treatment——'

'He doesn't need treatment. He's a doctor,' declared Sharon scathingly, drawing another impatient look from her husband. 'Con, I'm only trying to find out what's going on. D'you want to phone David?'

'I want you to go to work,' said Conor, in a low, controlled-voice, and Olivia could feel Sharon's hostility clear across the room. 'If it's necessary to phone Marshall, I'll do it.'

'Oh...' Sharon's mouth tightened. 'Well, if you're sure.'

Conor didn't say anything then. He just looked at her. But Olivia had the feeling that the message he was emitting was loud enough. Sharon evidently thought so too, because, after only a slight hesitation, she offered a brief word of farewell and departed. The sound of the outer door slamming was a flagrant indication of her feelings, however, and Olivia made a conspicuous effort to avoid Conor's knowing gaze.

It wasn't difficult. Her surroundings were so familiar that it was easy to find another outlet for her thoughts. Incredible as it seemed, little had changed in the eleven years since she was here last. The room had been re-decorated, of course, and the sofa, on which she was reclining so unwillingly, had been re-covered. But the tall cabinets that had contained Sally's collection of Waterford crystal were still there, along with the writing-desk in the window where Keith used to keep the accounts. Even the ornaments adorning the Victorian mantel were pieces Conor's parents had collected on their frequent trips to the Continent. They used to spend their summers camping in the south of France, she remembered. She had even gone with them a couple of times, when Conor was six or seven years old.

'I'll get the coffee,' he said now, as if realising she needed a few minutes to relax. 'I won't be long. I was making a pot before—well, before I saw you.'

Olivia didn't have time to think of a response before he had left the room. In any case, she was still stunned by the fact that the house had evidently not been sold, after all. Her grandmother had never mentioned it before she died, and Olivia had never thought to ask. But then, after moving into the nursing home, Mrs Holland had lost touch with many of her friends. She hadn't even attended Sally's and Keith's funeral.

Taking a deep breath, Olivia used her hands to ease herself to the edge of the sofa. Then, with some trepidation, she lowered her feet to the floor. Her leg still hurt, but the pain was bearable now. An indication that she was improving, she thought wryly. If only it had improved earlier, before she had got herself into this predicament.

'What are you doing?'

Conor's impatient voice arrested her appraisal of her condition. Not that it mattered really. There was no way she could leave here without his co-operation. Even if

she insisted on taking a taxi, she would have to use his
phone.

Now Conor came into the room carrying a tray bearing
two beakers, a cream jug, and a pot of coffee. Hooking
a low end-table with his foot, he positioned it near the
sofa, then set down his burden before subsiding on to
the seat beside her.

His weight brought a resulting depression in the
cushions, and Olivia had to grasp the arm of the sofa
closest to her to prevent herself from sliding towards him.
It was a timely reminder—if any were needed—that
Conor was no longer the skinny youth he used to be.
Without his jacket, which he had apparently shed somewhere between here and the kitchen, his upper torso was
broad and muscular beneath the knitted shirt he was
wearing. She couldn't help noticing his legs, too, as she
shuffled uneasily towards her end of the sofa. Spread as
they were, to allow him easy access to the coffee, one
powerful thigh was barely inches from the hand with
which she was supporting herself. She knew a momentary urge to spread her fingers over his thigh, but
happily that madness was only fleeting. It was just so
amazing to remember him as a child and compare that
image with the man he was now.

'Cream?' he asked abruptly, and Olivia blinked.

'Oh—no. Just black,' she said hurriedly. Maybe the
strongly flavoured brew would help to normalise the
situation. Just at the moment, she had a decided feeling
of light-headedness.

'So,' he said, after handing her the beaker of coffee,
'd'you want to tell me what you're doing here?'

Olivia cradled her cup between her palms, and cast
him a sideways glance. He wasn't looking at her at the
moment, and she was grateful. It gave her an opportunity to study his features without fear of appre-
hension, and she needed that. Dear God, she thought,
her gaze moving almost greedily over lean cheekbones,
a strong jaw, and a wide, thin-lipped mouth—she had

not dreamed he could be so familiar to her, not after all these years. But he was. Older, of course, and harsher; but essentially the same. She wondered how long he had been in England. Not too long, she guessed, judging by his tan. And those sun streaks in his sandy hair; he hadn't acquired them in this northern climate.

Conor finished pouring his own coffee, and Olivia quickly looked away. Concentrating her attention on the fireplace, she noticed the ashes lying in the grate. Although the house was centrally heated, someone had had a fire the night before. The image of Conor and his wife sharing this sofa in front of the open fire, even perhaps making love by firelight, flashed into her mind. It brought an uneasy prickling to her skin, and she angrily thrust it away. It was because she still thought of this as Sally's and Keith's house, she told herself grimly. And of Conor as a boy, when he was obviously a man.

'Well?' he prompted, and she was aware of him turning to look at her now. It made her glad she still had her coat wrapped about her. The honey-coloured cashmere hid a multitude of sins.

'Well,' she countered, turning his way, but not quite meeting his eyes. 'Small world, isn't it? Who'd have thought you'd come back to Paget?'

'Why shouldn't I?' Conor was curt. 'It's my home.'

'Yes, well—I didn't realise the house hadn't been sold until now.' She cast a determinedly casual look around the room. 'It's amazing. Everything looks the same.'

Conor's mouth compressed. 'Are you saying that when you came up here you didn't know it was my house?'

His tone was vaguely accusing, and Olivia's head swung back to him with some haste. 'Of course,' she exclaimed, meeting his green gaze half indignantly. She felt the warm colour surge into her throat at his cool appraisal. 'I—I just wanted to—to look around.'

'For old times' sake?'

'Yes.' The colour had reached her cheeks now, but she refused to look away. 'After all, you didn't tell me you'd come back to England. How was I supposed to know?'

Conor put down his cup. 'Point taken,' he conceded, lounging back against the cushions and propping one booted ankle across one twill-covered knee. 'I guess I didn't think you'd be interested. You haven't exactly kept me up to date with your affairs.'

Olivia dragged her gaze away and looked down into her cup. She was aware that her heart was beating far faster than it should have been, and, in spite of the cold day outside, she was sweating. She should have taken off her coat, she thought, though all she did was draw it more closely about her. She needed its comforting folds to disguise her trepidation.

'So,' she said, feeling obliged to make some comment, 'you're a doctor now.'

'Don't make it sound so unlikely.' Conor inclined his head. 'I told you what I wanted to do, when I came to see you in London. Actually, I'm still in training. I've decided I want to specialise in psychological disorders, so for the last six months I've been working at the drug rehabilitation unit in Witterthorpe.'

'I see.' Olivia was impressed. 'Did—er—did you do the rest of your training in England?'

'No.' Conor reached for his coffee again and took a drink. 'Uncle Philip had a heart condition. He died soon after I started medical school. I stayed on in the States until I'd finished at med. school, because that was what Aunt Elizabeth wanted. She'd been good to me, and I guess I owed her that much. When I came here, I began the extra training you need to get a full British qualification.'

Olivia absorbed this with a pang. So Philip Cox had died, too. Just another aspect of Conor's life that she had known nothing about. But she could understand that Elizabeth Cox would have found comfort in her nephew.

Philip had only fathered daughters, which was probably why Sally had left Conor in his care.

Her coffee was almost finished, and, surreptitiously testing her foot against the floor, Olivia decided she was strong enough to stand. But, when she replaced her cup on the tray and inched forward on the sofa, Conor's hand closed about her sleeve.

'We've talked about me,' he said, 'but you still haven't told me what you're doing in Paget. You mentioned that you're staying in the village. Would that be at Tom Drake's place? I had a word with him this morning, but he didn't mention he had a visitor.'

'Why would he?' Olivia moved her arm so that he was forced to release her. 'He doesn't remember me. My married name means nothing to him.'

'Ah, yes. Your married name.' Conor lowered his foot to the floor, and leant forward, his arms along his thighs. 'You're a married lady, aren't you? Is your husband with you? Am I going to get to meet him?'

'No.'

Suddenly, Olivia had no desire to tell Conor about the divorce. His intimation that they might see one another again unsettled her, and, for some reason she didn't choose to recognise, she didn't want his sympathy. So long as he believed she was still married, he couldn't get too close to her. Though why the idea of his getting close to her should disturb her so, she couldn't imagine.

'No?' Conor's eyes were uncomfortably intent. 'Why? You ashamed of me or something?'

'Don't be silly.' Olivia licked her dry lips. 'He's not here, that's all. He—I'm just taking a short holiday. On my own.'

'Recuperating,' suggested Conor quietly, and she hesitated only a moment before allowing a taut nod. 'So what happened?' he persisted. 'D'you want to talk about it?'

'So you can psychoanalyse me?' she taunted, needing to make light of what was threatening to become a seriously heavy development. 'No, thanks. I crashed my car, that's all. It's a common enough story. Nothing exciting, I'm afraid——'

'When?'

'When what?'

'When did you crash your car?' Conor was unnervingly direct.

'Oh . . .' Olivia shrugged. 'A little while ago. Eight or nine months, I think.' She took a steadying breath. 'Look, I must be going, I've got some phone calls to make.'

Conor didn't move. 'And that was when you smashed up your leg? Eight or nine months ago?'

'Well, I didn't do it by falling over,' she retorted, still trying to lighten the mood. 'Conor, it's been lovely seeing you again, and I'm sorry if I upset your wife——'

'My wife?' At last something she said had distracted him. He raked back his sun-bleached hair with a restless hand. 'Sharon's not my wife!'

'Oh!' Once again, Olivia could feel the heat flooding up under her skin. 'Well, your—er—girlfriend, then,' she muttered, getting determinedly to her feet. She swayed rather unsteadily on one leg, as she gauged the distance between the couch and the door. 'Please explain that I don't make a habit of this. I'd hate her to think I was spying on you!'

'Spying on us?'

Conor came to his feet with a lithe movement, successfully reminding her of his superior height and build. It hardly seemed possible that he had once cried on her shoulder, she thought. These days, he was almost a head taller than she was.

'Well, you know what I mean,' she mumbled now, wishing she had chosen a less emotive word to describe her position. 'I really was curious to see this house again. And the cottage, too, of course. It was just my luck that I slipped and fell at the wrong moment.'

'Or mine,' remarked Conor softly, looking down at her, and she wondered how he could imbue those words with such a measure of intimacy.

Heavens, he was good, she thought ridiculously, unable to sustain his warm, disturbing gaze a moment longer. It probably amused him to see how he could disconcert her. A delayed payment for the way she had bossed him about in his youth.

'Look—I've got to go,' she said, wishing he would get out of her way so that she had an unobstructed passage to the door. She didn't want him to carry her again. She didn't want him touching her.

'OK.' As if sensing her frustration, he moved aside, and Olivia limped heavily across the room. Her leg would support her now, just, but she was conscious of his eyes upon her. He was probably gauging the possible seriousness of her injury, she thought crossly. He was a doctor, after all. He would know how restricted her movements were.

'I'll get the car,' he said, as she reached the doorway, and Olivia had no choice but to let him do it.

'What about your appointment?' she protested, realising she should have asked to use the phone as soon as she got here. She could have had the coffee while she waited for a cab.

'Let me worry about that,' he replied, brushing past her to collect his jacket from the banister in the hallway, and she clutched the door frame at her back in an unconsciously defensive gesture.

Conor's car had been in the garage, which explained why Olivia had only seen Sharon's Peugeot in the drive. Conor reversed his mud-smeared Audi round to the front of the house where Olivia was waiting, and she was glad she had been able to negotiate the steps without him watching her.

'I can manage,' she insisted, when he would have got out to help her into the front of the car, and Conor sank back into his seat.

'It's no sin to need assistance,' he remarked drily, as she eased her leg into a more comfortable position, and she wondered why she felt so absurdly sensitive with him. If she wasn't careful, she was going to arouse his suspicions as to why that should be so, and she couldn't even explain it to herself.

She always felt a certain sense of trepidation when she got into a car these days. It wasn't that she hadn't driven since the accident. On the contrary, she had insisted on replacing the car she had wrecked with a new one almost immediately. An automatic, of course, which for some time lay idle in the garage. But lately she had gained in confidence, and only the fear of the car breaking down had deterred her from attempting the drive to Paget.

Conor drove well: fairly fast, but not uncomfortably so, and any lingering fears left her. He traversed the narrow streets and intersections with an ease that spoke of long familiarity, and she guessed he knew the place better than she did these days. And obviously, he was used to driving in this country. She realised she had been in danger of thinking him a stranger to Paget.

They arrived at the Ship Inn, in what seemed an inordinately short space of time, and Olivia's fingers tightened round her handbag. 'Well—thank you,' she murmured politely, glancing up at the wooded façade of the building. 'I appreci——'

'When can I see you again?'

Conor's husky enquiry cut into her careful words of gratitude, and when she turned her head she found he had turned at right angles to the wheel, his arm along the back of the seat behind her.

Olivia gave a nervous laugh. 'Oh, I don't think——'

'Why not?' His expression flattened. 'As we haven't seen one another for God knows how many years, don't you think we ought to at least share a meal, for old times' sake?'

Olivia swallowed. 'You don't want to have a meal with me!' she protested.

'Why not?' he repeated.

'Well... I was—your mother's friend, not yours. You don't have to feel any obligation towards me.'

Conor slumped lower in his seat. 'Who said anything about an obligation?'

'Even so——'

'Even so nothing. OK. You were like my aunt, right? If it pleases you to remember the relationship like that, then no problem. How about me taking my favourite "aunt" to dinner? Like tonight, maybe. If you've not got anything else on.'

'I can't tonight.'

The words just sprang from her tongue, the refusal as necessary to her as her independence had been earlier. But there was no way she was going to put herself through any more torment today—physical or otherwise.

'Tomorrow, then,' he said, without hesitation, and, to her dismay, his fingers began plucking at the scarf she wore about her shoulders. He had nice hands, she noticed unwillingly, long-fingered and capable, and brown, like the rest of him. Or the part of him she could see, she amended shortly, uncomfortably aware of where her thoughts were taking her. *God*! She shivered. What was the matter with her?

'I—don't know,' she muttered, wishing she had the strength to be more decisive. But the truth was that, in spite of everything, she wasn't totally convinced she didn't want to see him again. After all, she defended herself, he was Sally's son. Surely, it was what *she* would have wanted—for them to be friends. But it was the ambivalence of her feelings that troubled her. That, and the sure knowledge that nothing was as simple as it seemed.

Conor toyed with the patterned scarf between his fingers. 'Tomorrow,' he said, the warmth of his breath moistening her ear. 'I'll pick you up at seven o'clock. What do you say?'

'I...' Olivia opened her mouth to make some further protest, and then closed it again. His face was much nearer now, and although his eyes were averted she had an unhindered view of his long lashes. They were sun-bleached these days, she noticed, like his hair, but just as vulnerable as she remembered them. 'Oh—all right,' she gave in weakly, knowing herself for a fool, and when he lifted his head she was sure of it. There was nothing vulnerable in his gaze at all. His face was quite expressionless. Whatever she thought she had seen in his expression was just wishful thinking.

But then he smiled. 'Great,' he said, withdrawing his arm from the back of the seat, and thrusting open his door. Then, before she had a chance to forestall him, he had circled the car and opened her door, offering her his hand to help her out.

'I can manage,' she exclaimed, frustration giving way to irritation, as annoyance at her weakness overwhelmed her. She shouldn't have allowed any of this to happen, she thought angrily, aware that the frown that drew her dark brows together did nothing for her appearance. But she had had a chance to end this association here and now, and she had blown it. Now she was committed to a whole evening in the company of a man she hardly knew.

CHAPTER THREE

THE next day and a half dragged.

It wasn't, Olivia assured herself, that she was looking forward to the evening ahead with pleasure. On the contrary, every time she thought about it she was struck anew with how unnecessary it seemed. It wasn't as if they had anything in common these days, she thought frustratedly. The Conor of today bore no resemblance to the helpless youth he'd been.

No, what she really wanted to do was get it over with. They would have dinner—possibly here at the inn—and share a stilted exchange of news. She would tell him some of the more amusing cases she had dealt with—carefully omitting any reference to her marriage—and he would talk about his job at the rehabilitation unit, and perhaps explain the differences between treatment here and in the United States.

All incredibly polite—and incredibly boring, she thought fretfully, particularly for someone whose taste in women obviously ran to the more glamorous specimens of her species. Like Sharon Holmes, for example, she acknowledged, irritated that she could remember the girl's name so clearly.

And when, the following evening, she seated herself in front of her dressing-table mirror to apply her make-up, it was Sharon's face that persisted in filling her mind. Why was it that blondes always seemed to hog the lime-light? she wondered. Was it that blonde hair usually went with a peaches-and-cream complexion, so different from her own pale features?

Whatever the reason, she wasn't here to compete with Conor's girlfriend, she thought crossly. Her only desire was that he shouldn't be ashamed of her. And if that meant wearing a dress instead of trousers, and trying to tame her curly hair into a more sophisticated style, so be it. She owed it to herself to do the best she could.

The folds of the satin wrap she had put on after her bath parted as she leant towards the mirror. The cleavage it exposed was not as generous as it had once been, and she had never been over-endowed in that department. Now, the lacy bra she was wearing was hardly necessary. She had only put it on to satisfy a need.

Clutching the lapels together again, Olivia viewed her appearance without encouragement. There wasn't much she could do with dark eyes that seemed to fill her face, or improve about bone structure that was definitely angular. She supposed she could disguise the hollows in her cheeks with a cream foundation, and use a cherry lipstick to give colour to her mouth. Thank God her lashes were long and thick and didn't need mascara. She had never been particularly expert when it came to using cosmetics.

With the make-up applied, and her black hair coiled into a rather precarious knot on top of her head, she pronounced herself satisfied. Well, she would have to be, wouldn't she? she thought grimly, pulling the only dress she had brought with her out of the wardrobe. She looked older than she was, but what of it? At least she wasn't afraid of her maturity. People would probably think she was Conor's mother. Dear God, why had she let herself in for this?

The dress was a warm Laura Ashley print, in shades of russet, green and brown. Its main attraction to Olivia was that it had a high neck and long sleeves, and the hem was only a few inches off her ankles. With opaque black tights to complete her cover, Olivia was reasonably satisfied with the result. Low-heeled shoes were not un-attractive on someone of her height and slenderness, and she was glad that the days of precarious heels were a thing of the past.

It was a few minutes to seven when she looked at her watch, and she wondered what she ought to do. She supposed she should go downstairs and wait for him, but ought she to take her coat with her? She had spent a good half-hour that morning brushing the dried mud stains off it. But if she took it with her, would Conor see that as an indication that she expected him to take her out?

It was a problem. The last thing she wanted was for him to feel obliged to take her to some expensive restaurant. The food at the Ship was good and wholesome, if a little lacking in imagination, but it suited her. Yet if she appeared without her coat and she needed it it would mean another trip upstairs to collect it. Something she would much rather not have to do at present.

She was still prevaricating when the phone rang. It startled her, as much because she guessed who it would be as from any shock at the sound. But the thought that it might be Conor ringing to say he couldn't make it made her move quickly to answer it. Perhaps he'd had an emergency. Doctors were notoriously unreliable.

Picking up the receiver, she put it to her ear. 'Hello?'

'Liv?' Conor's voice was unmistakable. 'You ready?'

As I'll ever be, thought Olivia drily, but she answered in the affirmative.

'Good. D'you want me to come up and fetch you, or will you come down? I thought we might have a drink in the bar before we go.'

Before we go! Olivia grimaced. So, they *were* dining somewhere else, after all. 'I'll come down,' she said crisply, not wanting another exhibition of his high-handedness. He had insisted on seeing her up to her room the day before, and embarrassed her horribly. Only her frozen expression had deterred Mrs Drake from making some comment when she served her supper that evening, and the idea of having a drink with him now, in the bar, was not appealing. Perhaps she could persuade him that they'd be better off drinking somewhere else. If she could forestall him, before he ordered himself a drink...

'OK.'

Conor accepted her decision without argument, and Olivia hurriedly collected her coat and handbag. The sooner she got downstairs, the better, she thought. If she knew Tom Drake, Conor was unlikely to be left on his own for long.

Thankfully her leg was much better this evening. She hadn't ventured out of the inn since the previous morning, and the prolonged rest had done it good. Happily, the weather had remained cold and windy, with snow flurries, so she had not had to explain her reasons for missing her usual walk.

The low-ceilinged stairway came down into the narrow reception hall of the inn. There was a small kiosk, which opened off the Drakes' living quarters, where guests went to check-in, or collect their mail. There were doors to the tiny dining-room, and to the smoke-room and bar, the latter commandeered by locals at this time of the year. And as Olivia couldn't see Conor hanging about the hallway, she guessed he had joined them. After all, he was a local, she reflected, her spirits sinking at the thought.

Deciding that if she put her coat on she would at least look as if she was waiting to leave, Olivia slid her arms into the sleeves. Then, as there was no one about, she checked her wavy image in the smoked glass of a lantern. Oh, well, she thought wearily, she might as well get it over with.

But, when she entered the bar, she couldn't immediately see Conor. It was already fairly busy, probably due to the fact that most people were coming out early to avoid the icy roads later. But, although there were several people standing at the bar, he wasn't one of them, and it wasn't until he spoke her name that she turned her head and saw them.

Yes, *them*, she saw incredulously, as her eyes took in the fact that Conor was not alone. But it wasn't Tom Drake, who was sipping a glass of white wine, and shifting his weight from one foot to the other, beside Conor. It was Sharon Holmes, wide-eyed and sultry-lipped, wearing a short-jacketed scarlet suit that exposed most of her shapely legs.

Olivia could not have been more taken aback. In spite of what she had seen the day before, and their obvious familiarity with one another, she had never considered that Conor might bring his girlfriend tonight. It had been foolish, she saw with hindsight, to imagine his invitation had meant anything more than a token homage to duty. She had been his mother's friend, she had been around for most of his early life, and he felt sorry for her. She had embarrassed all of them by appearing out of the blue like that, so he had offered her dinner as a means of absolving his responsibility. He didn't really want to spend the evening in her company. In fact, he was just as reluctant as she was. How could she have thought otherwise?

Now he left his companion to come and greet her, but although she attempted to proffer a nervous hand he ignored it, and brushed his lips against her cheek. The odour of the shaving foam he had used invaded her nostrils, along with the distinctly masculine scent of his body, and she caught her breath. But she bore the salutation valiantly, and even managed a smile when he drew back.

'How's the leg this evening?' he asked softly, his words for her ears only, and she said, 'Better, thank you,' in a stiff tone that couldn't help but reveal her feelings. But what else could he expect? she thought tensely. She was still recovering from shock.

He looked even more attractive this evening, though his clothes were not as formal as she had expected. Probably because she was too accustomed to dining with older men, she reflected ruefully. After all, even Stephen had been almost ten years older than she was. None the less, Conor's button-down collar—worn without a tie, she noticed—and black corded trousers were decidedly casual. The fine wool jacket he was wearing with them was a sort of dusty green, and matched neither his shirt nor his trousers. Yet, for all that, the clothes suited him, accentuating still more the differences between them.

Now, as if afraid she was missing something, Sharon joined them, and Olivia felt as dowdy as a sparrow with two gorgeous birds of paradise. No, not a sparrow, a starling, she corrected drily. Sparrows were small and compact, not long-legged and ungainly.

'Hello, Mrs Perry,' she said, once again relegating Olivia to an older generation. 'Isn't it cold? I bet you wish you'd chosen the Caribbean for your holiday.'

Olivia's smile felt glued to her mouth. 'Oh—yes,' she murmured, wondering exactly what Conor had told Sharon about her. He had evidently mentioned that she was married. She just hoped he hadn't said too much about the crash.

'Let me get you a drink,' suggested Conor swiftly. 'You two can find somewhere to sit down.'

'I'm quite capable of standing,' said Olivia, well aware that they hadn't been occupying one of the wooden tables when she came in. She gave Conor a resentful look, and then looked away again. 'I'll have a gin and tonic, thank you. No ice.'

Conor inclined his head, and although he didn't say anything she sensed his indignation. Well, she thought defensively, she wasn't an *old* lady. Not as old as he was implying, anyway. He might mean well, but she didn't like it. Not when she already felt like the ripest gooseberry in the basket.

'Shall we sit down?' asked Sharon, after Conor had departed to get her drink, and Olivia sighed. Oh, what the hell? she thought; perhaps she was being foolish in refusing the opportunity to take her weight off her leg. She'd already had one experience of what could happen when she acted recklessly. Her present predicament was a direct result.

So, 'If you like,' she agreed offhandedly, and followed the girl to a table in the corner.

Sharon set her drink on the table in front of her, and then looked thoughtfully at her companion. 'Conor says you're a lawyer,' she remarked. 'That's not how you got to know Mrs Brennan, is it?'

Mrs Brennan! For a moment, Olivia didn't understand who she was talking about. Her thoughts had been so wrapped up with Conor and this awful situation that it took several seconds for comprehension to dawn.

'Oh—you mean Sally,' she said hurriedly, and Sharon gave a nod. 'No—I—as I believe I told you, my grandmother used to live next door. At number seventeen Gull Rise, I mean. I lived with her after my own parents died. That's how I met—all the Brennans.'

'I see.' Sharon studied her consideringly. 'So you've known Conor a long time.'

'A—fairly long time,' conceded Olivia reluctantly, realising that Conor had apparently been less loquacious than she'd thought. She endeavoured to change the subject. 'Do—er—do you work with Conor, Miss Holmes?'

'Heavens, call me Sharon!' She uttered a girlish laugh. 'Miss Holmes makes me sound so *old*!' She let the implications of this sink in, and then added carelessly, 'No, my friend and I run a boutique in Ashford. I don't think Conor likes career-minded women.'

Or intelligent ones either, thought Olivia maliciously, meeting the other woman's eyes, and glimpsing avidity in their depths.

'Oh—present company excepted, of course,' Sharon added, clapping a rueful hand over her mouth. 'But you're different, Mrs Perry. You're—well, you're sort of——'

'—older?' suggested Olivia pleasantly, deciding there was no point in antagonising Sharon needlessly. It wasn't

Sharon's fault she was here, after all. It wasn't Sharon's fault that Olivia had mistaken Conor's motives.

'Well, yes,' the girl was continuing now, and then rushed on, as though Olivia was a confidante, 'You wouldn't believe what Conor has to put up with, working with so many women. Women doctors, that is. The women patients get a fix on him, of course, but that's different. They're sort of dependent, aren't they? But some of those women medics are man-hungry!' She rolled her eyes. 'I don't know what causes it. I suppose hospitals have always been known for stuff like that. Life and death! It sort of brings you close to nature. Regular hotbeds of intrigue, aren't they?' she added, with a giggle. 'If you'll excuse the pun!'

Olivia shook her head. She had the feeling Sharon watched too many soap operas. 'Did—er—did Conor tell you that?' she enquired mildly, and the girl reached determinedly for her glass.

'Not in so many words,' she admitted, but her eyes were moving past Olivia, her lips parting to allow her tongue free access to her upper lip. 'Here's Con,' she added, somewhat unnecessarily, and Olivia's lips tightened. The girl's expression was as hungry as any man-hunter's at that moment, and she wondered if Sharon was really as ingenuous as her words would have her believe.

'One gin and tonic, as requested,' Conor announced, setting a glass containing a measure of gin in front of her. He delivered himself of the small bottle of tonic water to go with it, and then took the stool beside Sharon. He had got himself a drink, too, Olivia noticed. Orange juice, by the look of it, and her eyebrows lifted almost involuntarily. 'I'm driving,' he said, reading her expression all too easily. 'Cheers!' He lifted his glass towards her.

'Cheers,' Olivia echoed, adding a splash of tonic to the gin, and taking a generous mouthful. Perhaps she should have chosen something more innocuous, she reflected, aware that she was probably going to need to keep her wits about her this evening. But right then she needed the boost that only alcohol could give her.

'I've been telling Mrs Perry about the clinic,' said Sharon, not altogether truthfully, and Olivia guessed she was warning her against making some unwary comment. 'You wouldn't believe what people will do to get money to support their drug habit.' She smiled artlessly into Conor's eyes. 'Con's ever so patient with them. I sometimes think I should become one of his addicts myself. I might get more attention that way.'

Olivia didn't know where to look. Instead of returning Sharon's gaze, Conor had turned his eyes on her, and she wondered if he knew how uncomfortable she felt. But, of course, he must do, she thought bitterly, remembering how effortlessly he had read her thoughts before. He was probably enjoying this. Waiting to see how she would react to the situation.

But, to her surprise, it was Conor who saved her embarrassment. 'I'd guess Liv has to deal with enough drug-related offences, without wanting to spend the evening talking about them,' he remarked evenly. 'And call her Olivia, will you? She's not my mother!'

'Oh, thanks!'

Olivia's mollification was short-lived, as Conor's mouth curled into a most infuriating smile. The pig! He *was* enjoying this, she thought angrily, glaring at him. But one thing was certain. She was not going to pander to his ego.

'My pleasure,' he responded silkily, and Sharon put her glass back on the table with a decided snap.

'I've told—Olivia—about the boutique,' she intervened, obviously not enthusiastic about using the other woman's Christian name, but unwilling to be ignored. 'She might like to call in some time. We sell clothes to—to everyone.'

Including older women, appended Olivia drily, but at least Sharon's words had attracted Conor's attention.

'I'm sure Liv appreciates the offer, but I doubt she'll take you up on it,' he said. 'It's quite a trek to Ashford, and Liv doesn't drive.'

'Yes, I do.' Despite her misgivings, Olivia couldn't let him get away with that. 'I admit I haven't brought the car with me. But I do have one. In spite of everything,' she finished, a trifle smugly.

Conor's gaze was interrogative now. 'You've had approval from your doctor?'

'Yes.' Olivia took another swig of gin, resenting his implication.

'And it's an automatic, I presume?'

'Yes,' she said again. 'Really, Conor, I'm not an invalid! However disappointing that may be!'

It was an unforgivable thing to say, and she regretted it almost at once. Looking away towards the bar, where Tom Drake was leaning on the counter, chatting with one of his cronies, she wondered if she could just make some excuse and join them. Anything would be better than spending the evening fending off Sharon's spite and Conor's sympathy.

An uneasy silence had fallen now, and she was almost relieved when Sharon said, 'Oughtn't we to be leaving? You did say you'd booked the table for eight, didn't you, Con? And if the roads are slippy...'

'What? Oh—yes, I guess so.' Conor swallowed the remainder of the orange juice in his glass, and set it back on the table. He paused, and then said quietly, 'Are you ready, Liv? You can leave the rest of your drink, if you want to. We'll have some wine when we get to the Roundhouse.'

The Roundhouse. Olivia absorbed the name he had used without recognition. But, contrarily, she chose to empty the contents of her glass before rising, meeting his gaze with a defiant one of her own, because she didn't have an alternative.

If Sharon was aware of the undercurrent between them as they drove the three miles to the restaurant, she chose not to acknowledge it. Instead, she kept up an incessant chatter about the girl she worked with at the boutique, and other friends Conor seemed to know. And, as Olivia was ensconced in the back of the car, and didn't know any of these people anyway, her isolation was complete.

The Roundhouse turned out to be a converted windmill, whose stark white-painted façade belied the colourful warmth within. A mirror-backed bar adjoined the circular restaurant, and there was a comfortable air of bustle, and the delightful smell of good food.

Sharon hadn't brought an overcoat with her, but Conor suggested Olivia might like to leave hers in the cloakroom. It would be easier than having it draped over her chair all evening, and she was glad of the opportunity to escape for a few moments.

There were two women already in the cloakroom, chatting to the attendant, but Olivia was aware that their eyes were drawn to her as she limped across the floor. She was beginning to realise how frustrating it could be to be disabled. She wished people would just ignore her, or treat her like everyone else. She didn't want their sympathy. She didn't need it.

The face that looked back at her from the mirror was no more appealing. She should never have worn the cherry lipstick, she thought. It looked too bright and garish, and the speed with which she had downed the gin and tonic had brought an unnatural blush of colour to her cheeks. It wouldn't surprise her if Sharon thought she was having hot flushes, she brooded cynically. It would be all one with the way the girl was treating her. And she wasn't improving matters by acting like a shrew.

The truth was that she had got out of the habit of being in company, she admitted. Since the accident, she had tended to avoid social gatherings. Which was one of the reasons why returning to work had not been such a good idea. She seemed to have lost the ability to communicate with people. She needed a breathing space. A time for her mind to mend, as well as her body.

To her relief, the two women departed before she was ready to hand over her coat. And then, delivering it to the attendant, she discovered she had made another error of judgement. They hadn't been gossiping about her at all.

'Isn't it awful,' the attendant sighed, 'losing a child so young? I expect you heard that lady say her daughter had just died of leukaemia, didn't you? Only thirteen, she was. Poor woman. How do you get over something like that?'

Olivia made some suitable rejoinder, and emerged from the cloakroom feeling duly chastened. When she saw Conor and Sharon waiting for her by the bar she determined to be more positive. It wasn't their fault she wasn't enjoying the evening, she told herself. She was far too sensitive about herself, and they were bearing the brunt. She had to stop looking for trouble, and stop being so touchy.

'I've got you a glass of white wine,' Conor said now, handing it to her, and Olivia squashed the unworthy thought that he was treating her like Sharon. All the same, she couldn't help wondering if he doubted her ability to hold her liquor. Did he imagine she must have been tipsy to have made that insulting remark earlier?

With her mind about to hop on to the old tack, she remembered what she had promised herself as she came to join them. Conor had bought her a drink, that was all. She ought to be grateful. Besides, the wine was nice, and probably much better for her.

'Our table's almost ready,' said Sharon, checking one of the gold studs she wore in her ear with a scarlet-tipped finger. 'The food here's really special. You ought to try the watercress mousse. It practically melts in your mouth.'

'I may do that.' Olivia was pleased to hear her voice sounded reasonably friendly as she responded to Sharon's suggestion. 'Do you come here often? I suppose it's fairly handy.'

'Sometimes. If we don't feel like making a meal,' responded Sharon cosily, giving Conor an intimate smile. 'But we don't mind staying in, do we, Con? We don't need a lot of entertaining. We can entertain ourselves.'

'I'm sure you can.'

Olivia buried her nose in her glass and wished for the waiter to come and save her from herself. But dear God, did the girl have to be so obvious? They lived together. Conor had as good as said as much. So what of it? It didn't mean anything to her.

To her relief, her prayers were answered, the dark-coated *maître d'* arrived at that moment to escort them to their table near the window. In the polite process of choosing where each of them was going to sit, Olivia was able to relax, and she was happy to use the excuse of studying the menu to avoid any further eye-contact with Conor.

But when their orders had been taken there was nothing to prevent him from looking directly at her, and she wondered if it had been such a good idea to avoid the seat next to his. And, in an effort to try and restore the conversation to a more casual footing, she determinedly asked him how his aunt was, and whether she still lived in Florida.

'Still in the same house,' agreed Conor, lounging indolently in his chair. 'We're a consistent family. We like familiarity. And my aunt has a lot of friends in Port Douglas.'

'I'm sure.' Olivia ignored the reproof, and persevered, 'I suppose your cousins are married now. Do they live in Port Douglas, too?'

'One of them does,' Conor conceded evenly. 'The other lives in California. But they come home fairly regularly. It's a big house. There's lots of room.'

'And I suppose you go home fairly regularly, too,' Olivia ventured, feeling a little more confident, but when she lifted her head Conor's expression was less than encouraging.

'Paget is my home,' he declared, his eyes as cool as ice-floes. 'Why else d'you think I wanted to keep the house?'

'Well...' Olivia shrugged. 'I thought—after living in the United States for so many years——'

'Only nine years, Liv. I've been back in England for quite some time. I was a resident at a hospital in London, before I came back to Paget.'

Olivia licked her dry lips. 'Oh! I didn't know.'

'How could you? You were too busy with your own life.' Conor almost made it sound like a criticism. 'So, tell us,' he continued, 'what does your husband do for a living?'

Olivia hesitated. Knowing what she did about Conor, there was no earthly reason why she should choose to keep her divorce a secret any longer. But the idea of confessing her inability to sustain a relationship to Sharon brought an unwelcome tightness to her throat.

'He—I—a sales manager,' she got out jerkily, immediately ashamed of her dishonesty. 'He—works for an electrical manufacturer,' she added, when it became apparent that something more was needed. 'Food processors, blenders, that sort of stuff.'

'Ooh, I bet you have all the latest gadgets in your kitchen,' exclaimed Sharon, half enviously, and Olivia felt even worse.

'Not necessarily,' she mumbled, and once again she was saved from further embarrassment by the arrival of the wine waiter. The discussion that ensued erased any further need to elaborate, and happily Sharon seemed to prefer talking about her own affairs to anyone else's.

The food lived up to Sharon's prediction, and although Olivia found it difficult to do it justice she couldn't deny that the delicate mousse and juicy steak were every bit as delicious as she could wish. But, even though Sharon monopolised Conor's attention for most of the meal, her appetite was practically non-existent. In consequence, she drank rather more of the fine claret Conor had ordered than perhaps she should have done, and when they rose from the table her unsteadiness wasn't wholly the result of her injury.

As though sensing her uncertainty, Conor moved round the table to put his hand beneath her elbow, and although Olivia cast him an indignant look she couldn't deny she needed his support. Just till she got her balance, she told herself, as his strong fingers bit into her arm. He probably resented having to do this just as much as she did.

'Go get Olivia's coat, Sharon,' Conor ordered, as soon as they reached the foyer, and although it obviously wasn't a popular request the girl didn't argue.

'I could have got it myself,' protested Olivia, after the young woman had departed clutching the redemption ticket. She endeavoured to move away from him. 'Thank you. I can manage now.'

'Can you?' Conor didn't look convinced.

'Yes.' Olivia jerked her arm out of his grasp and backed away. 'I wish you'd stop behaving as if I shouldn't be out without a keeper!'

'Stop exaggerating, Liv!' Conor's mouth compressed. 'All I did was hold your arm.'

'Because you thought I was in danger of showing you up!' retorted Olivia hotly. 'Well, don't worry, Conor. I won't let it happen again.'

'No?'

'No.' Olivia glanced swiftly around to make sure their conversation was not being overheard, and then added grimly, 'I'm sure you'll be as glad when this evening is over as I will. It was kind of you to invite me, but I think you'll agree it was a mistake!'

Conor's face darkened, but Sharon's return prevented him from making a reply. Which was just as well, thought Olivia ruefully, as the doorman helped her to put her coat on. Judging from his expression, it would not have been anything good.

The journey back to the Ship was accomplished
without incident. Even Sharon had little to say, beyond
commenting on how full she felt. She was looking
forward to going to bed, she added. She felt *so* sleepy.
But not too sleepy, Olivia hazarded, with a cynical twist
to her lips.

However, when they arrived at the inn, Conor turned
off the car's engine. 'I won't be long,' Olivia heard him
say to Sharon, as she was levering herself out on to the
pavement, and she caught her breath. Dear heaven, she
thought, surely he wasn't going to insist on seeing her
up to her room tonight? Not with his girlfriend waiting,
and the car in danger of losing its heat.

She was standing beside the car when he came round
to join her, and although their last words had hardly
been cordial she strove for a friendly tone.

'Thank you—both of you—for the evening,' she murmured, aware that Sharon had lowered her window to
hear what was said. 'It's been lovely——'

'I'm glad to hear it,' responded Conor, and she wondered if only she could hear the irony in his voice.
Ignoring her resistance, he turned her forcefully towards
the building. 'Let's go, hmm? It's bloody cold out here.'

Olivia glared at him, but he had her at a disad-
vantage, and he knew it. So, instead of fighting him,
she cast a helpless smile in Sharon's direction. 'Goodnight,' she called, with rather more warmth than she had
shown the girl thus far. 'I won't keep him.'

Fortunately the lobby was empty, though there was
plenty of noise coming from the bar, and Olivia was
able to wrench her arm from Conor's grasp. 'Don't do
this to me,' she warned, but he followed her up the stairs
anyway, and by the time she reached her door she was
panting from exertion.

'All right,' she said, backing up against the door as
he loomed over her, his shadow elongated by the light
from the stairs. 'Now will you leave? You've done

everything you possibly can to humiliate me. So please, just—go away.'

'How?'

'How what?' Olivia was confused.

'How have I humiliated you?' asked Conor, propping his shoulder against the wall beside her. 'What did I do?'

'What did you...?' Olivia broke off and gripped the handle of the door behind her, wishing she could just slip inside without further argument. 'Look—I really don't want to talk about it. Can't we just say goodnight? I—just want to go to bed.'

Conor frowned, then he put out his hand and lifted a tendril of dark hair that had fallen beside her ear. 'Are you mad because I brought Sharon?' he asked softly, and Olivia was so shocked she was sure she must have misheard him.

'I—beg your——'

'I thought it might make things easier for you,' he added, as she turned horrified eyes in his direction. 'You seemed so nervous of me yesterday morning, and I guess I was a little nervous myself. I've thought about how I'd feel seeing you again after so long, and I was so afraid of screwing up!'

Conor? Afraid? Olivia couldn't believe it. 'Oh, really,' she began, but he wouldn't let her continue.

'I mean it,' he said, his hand dropping to the belt that rode low on his hips. 'Hear me out. Please.'

Olivia shrugged. 'All right.' She was purposely not looking at him, but she couldn't help watching those strong supple fingers easing their way under the taut leather. She was suddenly aware that she was wondering how they would feel touching her. And, although she stifled the thought instantly, its memory remained.

'I know I always say the wrong thing,' he muttered now, and she was aware of his eyes moving over her face. 'Hell, don't I?' he added. 'Tell me about it. And I know your opinion of me is coloured by the way I behaved that time I came to see you in London, but I can't do anything about that. Honestly, Liv, you don't know how much I've regretted mouthing off as I did. I was just a stupid idiot, and if I hurt your feelings, then believe me, I'm sorry.'

Olivia took a deep breath. 'Conor, it really doesn't matter that much——'

'Yes, it does.' As if he couldn't help himself, his fingers moved to straighten the lapel of her coat. 'Liv, I wanted us to start afresh. I wanted us to be friends.'

Olivia lifted her shoulders. 'We are friends——'

'Are we?'

'Yes.' Olivia was beginning to feel the strain of standing in one position for too long, but it wasn't just her physical discomfort that made her add swiftly, 'Honestly, Conor, I've forgotten all about that time in London.' It was a lie, but he was not to know that. 'Heavens, it was years ago. Now, don't you think you ought to go? I'm sure Sharon must be getting very impatient——'

'So, you'll let me see you again?'

'What?' Olivia caught her breath. 'Oh, I—I don't think so.'

'Why not?' He looked down into her anxious brown eyes, and, before she could stop him, he had cupped her face in his hand. 'If we're friends,' he reminded her roughly. His eyes darkened, and as his fingers moved against her flesh she could feel their hard pressure clear down to her toes. 'Hot damn, I wish you weren't married,' he groaned suddenly, and, bending his head, he brushed her parted lips with his mouth.

CHAPTER FOUR

AT TWO o'clock the next morning, Olivia got up to take a sleeping pill. Staring at her reflection in the mirror above the wash-basin in the bathroom, she tried to get what had happened into perspective. But she couldn't. She was too tired—and too confused—to make any sense of it at all.

Why had Conor kissed her? As she fished one of the capsules out of the bottle, she acknowledged that that was the real reason she was finding it so difficult to sleep. His action had taken her completely by surprise, and while she was sure she was exaggerating its importance, the fact remained that he had kissed her mouth.

Filling a glass with water, she chided herself for allowing him to disconcert her like this. Heavens, she thought, as she tossed the capsule to the back of her throat and swallowed it with a gulp of the ice-cold water, it wasn't as if it was anything out of the ordinary. Men and women kissed all the time. In the circles she moved in, it was an accepted form of salutation between the sexes.

But it was the way he had kissed her that troubled her most. She was almost convinced she had felt his tongue probing her lips. God! She had been as shocked as a virgin on her first date. And when he'd made that crack about wishing she was single she'd felt as guilty as any cheating wife.

Her stomach heaved as the water churned up the mixture of gin and wine she had drunk earlier. The alcohol was probably responsible for her feeling so over-stimulated, she reflected. Her body was tired, but her brain wasn't getting the message.

She crawled back into bed, and tried to tuck her freezing toes into the hem of her nightshirt. She was so cold, in spite of the thick quilt that covered her. Sharon wouldn't have that problem. Not with Conor's muscled body coiled around her...

Dammit!

Olivia shifted crossly on to her other side. Where had that thought come from? For heaven's sake, she wasn't jealous of the girl, was she? Just because Conor had kissed her, surely she wasn't allowing herself to think she had some claim to his affections? Dear lord, he was only a boy! Thinking of him as anything else was—was ridiculous!

But he wasn't a boy, a small voice reminded her drily. He was a man, in every sense of the word, and an attractive one at that. No wonder Sharon had said those women at the clinic hung on his every word. It would be incredibly easy to be seduced by his lazy eyes and smiling mouth.

But not for her, she chided herself fiercely. She wasn't like those other women. She was just someone who had known his mother, and because of that he felt a certain closeness to her. But it wasn't the kind of closeness he had with Sharon. It had no—sexual—connotation.

She pressed her hand to her throat. Just thinking about him with Sharon brought an unpleasant tightness to her breasts, and she was aware of them peaking against the soft cotton. The abrasion was unwelcome, and she ran her hand half impatiently down her body, trying to soothe her perverse flesh. But her arousal stemmed from another part of her body, and she rolled on to her stomach to try and subdue its craving.

All the same, the knowledge that she could feel like this, with so little provocation, was alarming. In spite of the fact that it was almost two years since she and Stephen had shared a bed, she had never before felt she was missing anything. On the contrary, she had grown used to regarding herself as a dispassionate woman. That

was why she was so good at her job. And, although she
had never objected to Stephen's lovemaking, she had felt
no great eagerness for it either.

Which was why what was happening to her now was
so disturbing. It was like shedding a layer of skin, and
finding a stranger underneath. She didn't recognise
herself, and she wasn't sure she wanted to. It was safer
to stay immune from the hungers of the flesh.

Nevertheless, when she awakened the next morning it
was to discover that the problem hadn't gone away. Not
that that was so surprising really. She had spent what
was left of the night in a haze of heat and sweat, and
sexual frustration. But one thing was certain: she had
to get herself under control before she saw Conor again.
She would hate him to find out that his careless kiss had
caused such an emotional furore inside her.

A cool shower worked wonders, and by the time she
had pulled on a pair of dark green leggings and a thigh-
length sweater and brushed her unruly hair into a severe
knot she was almost convinced she had been exaggerating. The mind was a funny thing, she thought, following Mrs Drake's ample form across the tiny dining-
room later. It was open to suggestion—even self-deceit.

'Oh—there was a phone call for you earlier,' Mrs
Drake exclaimed, after Olivia was seated. She pulled an
apologetic face. 'I almost forgot. It was young Dr
Brennan.'

'Was it?' Olivia could feel the familiar warmth en-
veloping her. What price self-deception now?

'Yes.' Mrs Drake folded her hands across her midriff.
"Course, Tom put the call through to your room, but
you didn't answer. I said to him, I did, you must be in
the shower. Can't hear that phone ringing when the water's running, and that's a fact.'

'I see.' Olivia was grateful for the warning. 'Um—did
he leave a message?'

'Only that he'd ring again later,' declared Mrs Drake ruefully. 'Sounded real disappointed, he did. Have—er—have you two known one another long?'

Olivia looked down at her place mat, with its black and white lithograph of the Romney, Hythe and Dymchurch railway. This was what she had been afraid of, of course. So far, she had managed to maintain her anonymity, but Conor's intervention had given her inquisitive landlady an opening.

'Quite long,' she replied at last, pretending to be interested in the morning newspaper. She glanced up as Mrs Drake still stood there, miming surprise. 'Just toast and coffee, as usual, please.'

It was hardly polite, and in other circumstances she would never have been so abrupt, but Mrs Drake was far too garrulous to confide in. However, she had bargained without taking the other woman's persistence into consideration. 'Had dinner with him and young Sharon last night, didn't you?' she declared, flicking a speck of dust from the table with the hem of her apron. 'Nice girl, Sharon. Her mother and me went to school together. Connie Simmons, as was. Family lived over towards Witterthorpe. Her mother's an auxiliary at the clinic where Dr Brennan works.'

'Really?'

The coolness of Olivia's tone was in direct opposition to the turmoil of her thoughts. Somehow, she hadn't thought of Sharon as having a family living locally. She had assumed they'd met while Conor was working in London. She hadn't imagined their relationship was so short-lived.

'Yes—well . . .'

Mrs Drake shrugged, and, evidently deciding her guest was unlikely to be any more forthcoming, she ambled away. But, when she was alone, Olivia put the newspaper aside, and gazed unseeingly out of the window. Of course, she could be wrong. Conor could have known Sharon since they were at school, too. She wondered how long they had been living together. And how serious the affair was.

Deciding she was becoming far too interested in Conor and his concerns, after breakfast Olivia collected her coat from her room and left the inn. She didn't tell the Drakes where she was going. And if Conor rang again they would have to tell him she still wasn't answering her phone. But right now, she needed some fresh air. A leisurely stroll across the marsh sounded very appealing.

The path took her over the sand-dunes, where clumps of tussocky grass held out against the encroaching sea, and out across the salt marshes, where sandpipers and herring gulls scavenged for food. It was a crisp morning—bright, but cold—and, beyond the break-water, the channel lay as still as a mill-pond. But, in spite of the lack of wind, the air was chilling, and even with her gloved hands tucked securely into her pockets Olivia could feel its bite.

But her leg felt much better, and she was relieved. Despite her restless night, a couple of days without any undue exertion had restored its fragile strength. Oh, she still had a bruise or two here and there, to add to her other scars. But nothing incapacitating, as she had first imagined.

She returned to the inn at lunchtime feeling considerably more optimistic. She had managed to pass the whole morning without thinking about Conor, or worrying what she was going to do about him. She had determinedly emptied her mind of all her personal problems, and even the prospect of returning to London didn't give her the sinking feeling it usually did.

'Did you have a nice walk, Mrs Perry?' Mrs Drake called from the reception kiosk as Olivia headed for the stairs, and she turned back good-naturedly.

'Very nice, thank you,' she replied, taking off her glove to push an unruly strand of hair out of her eyes. Then, deciding there was no point in resenting the woman's curiosity, she added, 'I went as far as the lighthouse. It was exhilarating.'

'Yes.' Mrs Drake smiled. 'You like your walks, don't you, Mrs Perry? Oh—before I forget, you had another call while you were out.' And, as Olivia stiffened, she fished a scrap of paper off the desk and held it out to her. 'I think it was your husband. Anyway——' she watched avidly as it was read '—he's left you a number where you can reach him.'

Olivia caught her lower lip between her teeth. Sure enough, the number was familiar to her. It was the number of Stephen's mobile phone. The one he never went anywhere without. As if she would ever forget it, she thought bitterly. But how had he known where to find her?

'Would you like me to dial the number for you?' suggested Mrs Drake hopefully, and Olivia guessed she was dying to know what was going on. After all, she had been staying at the inn over a week now, and so far she had had no contact with her husband.

'I'll ring him later,' Olivia murmured now, stuffing the scrap of paper into her pocket. And then, before she could stop herself, 'Um—that's all, is it? There weren't any other calls?'

'Dr Brennan didn't ring again, if that's what you mean,' declared Mrs Drake immediately, and Olivia thought how conspicuous she was, being the only guest. 'I expect he's busy with his patients. A queer lot some of them are, risking their health with heroin and suchlike. Can't see any sense in it myself. What's the point of injecting yourself with drugs to get some passing thrill, when most times they're too zonked out to enjoy it?'

Olivia gave a rueful smile. 'I really don't know,' she said, deciding there was no advantage to be gained in arguing the point. To hear the finer details of human need and social deprivation was not what Mrs Drake wanted from her. Besides, Olivia had no desire to get into a discussion where the particulars of her personal involvement became an issue.

She had started for the stairs again, when Mrs Drake called her back. 'Will you be wanting lunch, Mrs Perry?' she asked expectantly, and Olivia's breath escaped on a sigh.

'I—yes. Yes, in about fifteen minutes,' she agreed, grasping the gnarled banister with a determined hand.

'That'll give you time to make your call,' observed her landlady irrepressibly. 'It's steak and kidney pudding. Just what you need on a day like this.'

Olivia managed a smile, and then set off up the stairs, before Mrs Drake could think of anything else. It was ironic, really, but they had had more conversation in the last few hours than they had had in the whole of the past week. Olivia hoped it wasn't going to become a habit. She was too private a person these days to enjoy talking about herself.

Of course, she thought, as she shed her coat in her bedroom, Conor knew plenty about her now, and if he told Sharon, and Sharon told her mother... But no. Olivia refused to consider what might happen in that eventuality. If things became too awkward, she could always go somewhere else.

Still, sitting down to a plate of steaming steak and kidney pudding some time later, she hoped it wouldn't come to that. Until she had taken that ill-advised sojourn into the past, she had been enjoying her stay at the inn. Even if she had been born somewhere else, Paget was where she had her roots. She mustn't allow her unwelcome awareness of Conor to influence her actions.

In any case, at the moment, she decided she was more concerned with why Stephen should be trying to get in touch with her. It was months since she had seen him, months since they had had any communication, except via their respective solicitors. She hoped there was no hiccup over the finalising of their divorce. She wanted it to be done with. She wanted to be free.

The newspaper she had left by her plate at breakfast-time was still there, and she propped it against the salt and pepper shakers as she dipped her fork into the rich concoction of meat and vegetables on her plate. It tasted as delicious as it looked, and, in spite of her anxieties about Stephen, she was hungry. With the local news for company, she ate more enthusiastically than usual, only lifting her head when a shadow fell across the table.

She had expected it to be Mrs Drake, and she was getting ready to compliment her on the pudding, when she realised the intruder was not female. Leather brogues, a beige suit whose trousers needed pressing, and a flapping trench coat all added up to a masculine presence, and, for all she hoped it wasn't so, she wasn't really surprised when her eyes travelled up to her husband's triumphant face.

'May I join you?' he asked, already pulling out a chair, and seating himself opposite. 'Long time no see.'

'What are you doing here, Stephen?'

Olivia could barely keep the indignation out of her voice. She was already imagining what Mrs Drake would make of this, and the thought of her asking if he was staying the night, and having to explain that they didn't share a room any more, filled her with dismay. So much for keeping her affairs private, she reflected impatiently. What did he think he was doing?

'Don't sound so pleased to see me. I might get a swelled head,' he remarked now, easing his trench coat off his shoulders, and picking up the menu card. 'What's the food like here? What you're eating smells good.' He looked across at her, and his eyes moved speculatively over her face, noting the becoming colour her walk had given her, and approving the brightness of her eyes. 'I must say, it seems to be agreeing with you. You look good, Ollie, really good.'

'Don't call me Ollie,' she said, between her teeth. 'And how did you know where I was? I didn't even tell Mr Halliday my address.'

Stephen tapped his nose with a smug finger, and Olivia knew a growing sense of resentment that he should think he had the right to come here and disrupt her holiday. All right, so Paget wasn't everybody's idea of a relaxing location. That didn't alter the fact that she had chosen it because she wanted to be alone.

Mrs Drake's appearance was inevitable. Viewing her two guests with evident satisfaction, she made her way purposefully to their table, her face beaming. 'Will the gentleman be wanting lunch, too, Mrs Perry?' she asked, her eyes missing nothing of Stephen's appearance. 'This wouldn't be the gentleman that phoned earlier, would it? Oh—pleased to meet you, Mr Perry. I'm Mrs Drake.'

Olivia sat there, helpless, letting Stephen introduce himself with a feeling almost of disbelief. This couldn't be happening, she thought incredulously. She and Stephen had nothing more to say to one another. Their marriage was over. How dared he come here now and disrupt her privacy?

But, watching him practise his charm on Mrs Drake, she knew Stephen was completely indifferent to her feelings. He always had been. She should have divorced him long ago. She had only been fooling herself by imagining she could have ever made it work.

She couldn't even imagine what she had ever seen in him, these days. Of course, he was older than when she had married him—they both were—but the preceding years had not been exactly kind to Stephen. His hair was getting quite thin on top, and the belly, which spoke of too many liquid lunches, was beginning to bulge above his waistband. He looked what he was: a middle-aged travelling salesman, who had spent too many years on the road.

When Mrs Drake departed to get him a helping of the steak and kidney pudding, Olivia could hold back no longer. 'I don't know what you've come here for, Stephen,' she said, 'but, whatever it is, you're wasting your time. I'd like you to leave. As soon as possible.

Before Mrs Drake comes back would suit me very well. Don't worry about paying for your food. I'd consider it a privilege.'

'Oh, Ollie!' The reproachful diminutive grated on her nerves. 'What a way to treat your husband!'

'You're not my husband,' retorted Olivia, glad they were the only occupants of the dining-room. 'Stephen,' she sighed, 'don't you think this is rather silly? The last time I saw you—in the hospital, wasn't it?—you couldn't wait to exempt yourself from any responsibility for me.'

Stephen's face suffused with colour. 'That's not true, Ollie. You wanted the divorce, not me. And—and when you were at death's door, so to speak, I wanted to do anything I could to aid your recovery.'

Olivia's mouth compressed. 'Oh, really?'

'Yes, really.' Stephen seemed to gain confidence from affirming this belief. Indeed, she realised, he had a positive flair for self-deception. 'I would have cared for you, if that were what you'd wanted. But the doctors said your condition was critical, and I did what I could to relieve it.'

'Oh, Stephen!' The disgust was evident in Olivia's voice. 'Stop deluding yourself. You were shocked out of your mind when you saw my injuries. And an invalid wife was the last thing you wanted. Be honest for a change. It suited you to pull the plug.'

'Well, you're not an invalid now, are you?' he exclaimed, and Olivia blinked. 'As a matter of fact, you've never looked better. Losing weight obviously suits you. If you didn't wear your hair tugged back like that, you'd look a proper stunner.'

'Stephen!'

'Well, I've always thought you were a good-looking woman,' he replied defensively. 'I wouldn't have married you if I hadn't been attracted to you. No, I—regret what happened to us. We were a good couple. And old man Darcy always liked you.'

'Did he?' Olivia didn't know how she kept her temper, but she did. 'However,' she continued thinly, 'the opinion your boss has—or had—of me isn't an issue here——'

'But it is.' Stephen broke into her words, to lean across the table. 'It is an issue, Ollie. He—well, he's not at all happy about the divorce. He likes his salesmen to be married. He says it keeps their minds on the business, if you see what I mean.'

Olivia's breath gurgled in her throat. 'As you did, you mean?' she exclaimed chokingly, realising she could actually laugh at what had happened now. The whole affair seemed ludicrous in retrospect, and Stephen's part in it no more than he deserved.

'That wasn't funny,' he declared now, his rather full face mirroring his indignation. 'Just because I made a mistake——'

'*A* mistake?' broke in Olivia scornfully. 'Don't you mean a whole handful of them? Come on, Stephen. I may have been gullible once, but not any longer.'

Mrs Drake's reappearance with his lunch was an untimely interruption as far as Olivia was concerned. She had hoped, rather futilely, she realised, that she might have persuaded him to leave before the landlady returned. It also gave him a breathing space, and that irritated her, too. There was no way he could convince her that his motives for being here were anything more than selfish. And if he thought he had a chance of persuading her to think again at this late date he was more stupid than he looked.

Besides, why would he want to? She didn't believe that rubbish about Harry Darcy objecting to the divorce any more than she believed that Stephen was still attracted to her. It was possible that the company preferred its executives to be family men, but no one in this day and age was likely to balk if a marriage wasn't working. Least of all Harry Darcy, who had been married twice himself.

'Will—er—will your husband be staying overnight?' enquired Mrs Drake chattily, setting the meal and the

pint of lager Stephen had ordered on the table in front
of him.

'No...'

'Yes.'

They answered simultaneously, and, although Olivia
had intended to go on and explain that Stephen would
be leaving after lunch, his response left her speechless.

'Oh, then I'll have Dory change the sheets,' declared
the landlady happily. 'It'll do Mrs Perry good to have
some company, sir. Not much to do in Paget at this time
of the year. But I expect you know that, seeing as how
you and your wife have friends in the area.'

Now it was Stephen's turn to look confused, but Olivia
had no intention of enlightening him. She was too in-
furiated by his audacity to care what he thought. 'No,
don't bother changing the sheets, Mrs Drake,' she replied harshly, finding her voice. 'We don't sleep together.
We don't even share the same room!'

'Oh...' The woman was taken aback. 'Is that right?'
She looked to Stephen, as if for confirmation, and Olivia
wondered how she kept herself from screaming.

'Yes, that's right, Mrs Drake,' she insisted, glaring at
Stephen so threateningly that it would have taken a
stronger man than him to defy her wrath. '*If* Mr Perry
is staying—and I don't think he's made up his mind yet—
I'm afraid you'll have to find him alternative
accommodation.'

Stephen's mouth briefly took a sullen slant, and he
took a hefty swallow of the lager. Then, wiping his mouth
on the back of his hand, he tore his eyes away from
Olivia's angry face, and looked up at the landlady with
a winning smile. 'I'm afraid my wife's right, Mrs Drake,'
he said ruefully, and Olivia's nails dug into her palms
at his reproachful grimace. 'We don't share a room these
days. After the accident, her leg was in such a bad way
that the doctors advised me not to take any chances. I
might have bumped it, you see. And I didn't want to
hurt her. Unfortunately,' he went on, ignoring Olivia's

horrified expression, 'she's got used to sleeping alone. I am hoping to get her to change her mind, but for the time being...'

He allowed the sentence to tail away, and Mrs Drake looked just as sympathetic as he had intended. But Olivia's feelings about this were nothing compared to her fury at his mention of the accident, and it was no surprise when the landlady seized her chance.

'There, now,' she said, turning to her other guest. 'I said to Tom, I did, "Mrs Perry's got some sort of problem with her leg." And now you say you've had an accident. Well, I can't say I didn't suspect as much.'

Olivia pressed her lips together. Then, realising Mrs Drake's imagination was likely to run riot if she refused to answer, she said stiffly, 'I was involved in a car crash, that's all. Nothing too dramatic, I can assure you.'

'All the same...' Mrs Drake shook her head. 'No wonder you looked so peaky when you got here. Mind you, you're looking a lot better this morning. I said to Tom a few minutes ago, "Mrs Perry's got some colour in her cheeks again."'

'Exactly what I've been saying myself,' remarked Stephen smugly, and Olivia wondered why she didn't just tell the landlady about the divorce, and be done with it. But to do so now would mean she would have to admit she had been lying earlier. Oh, why hadn't she refused to speak to him, instead of making herself a liar by omission?

'Yes, well, I dare say seeing you again has helped,' Mrs Drake declared, looking approvingly at Olivia's almost empty plate. 'I see you enjoyed your lunch, Mrs Perry. Now, can I get you anything else before I go?'

'Nothing.' If the woman thought she was less than gracious, Olivia couldn't help it. She just wanted her to go so she could tell Stephen exactly what she thought of him. How dared he put her in this invidious position?

But when Mrs Drake had gone, it was Stephen who broke the silence. 'Looks like you're stuck with me,' he said, forking a huge amount of food into his mouth. 'I gather you haven't told anyone here that we're getting a divorce. Well, that suits me just fine——'

'Stephen!' Olivia's voice had risen several octaves, and it was with an immense effort that she toned it down again. 'What are you doing here? What do you want from me? You can't seriously imagine that I would take you back!'

Stephen shovelled another wedge of pudding into his mouth, and then regarded her as he chewed. 'I could say we're not divorced yet, Ollie,' he remarked, as soon as his mouth had emptied sufficiently for him to speak. 'If I was to tell your solicitor that you and I had had a reconciliation——'

'But we haven't. And we won't,' retorted Olivia, getting awkwardly to her feet. 'Don't threaten me, Stephen. Just at this moment, you've got more to lose than I have.'

'Oh, Ollie!' Putting down his fork, Stephen's expression underwent a complete change. Instead of aggression, his face took on a look of weary contrition, and, before she could avoid it, his hand had clutched her sweater. 'Must we have a slanging match? We loved one another once. Can you honestly say that that's all over?'

'Yes.' Olivia was unmoved. 'Stephen, if you care anything for me at all, you'll finish your lunch and then get out of here. I don't want to see you; I don't want to talk to you. And if you want to stop me hating you, you'll forget you ever came here.'

Stephen expelled his breath heavily. 'I can't do that, Ollie.'

Olivia dragged her sweater out of his grasp. 'Then I will!' she stated grimly, and started for the door.

'I can still *say* we had a reconciliation,' Stephen's voice called after her. 'It might not do any good, but are you willing to take that chance?'

Olivia halted. 'You bastard,' she exclaimed, turning back.

'No, I'm just desperate,' replied Stephen, glancing at her over his shoulder. 'Look, if you'll come back and sit down, I'll tell you what's happened.'

'I don't care what's happened.' Olivia was desperate, too.

'Not even if I tell you that if you just help me this one time I won't do anything to jeopardise the divorce?'

Olivia's shoulders sagged. She had seen enough messy divorces to know that judges were not always objective if a defendant was convincing enough.

'Why should I believe you?' she asked, hating herself for even listening to him.

'I don't see that you have a lot of choice,' he retorted, and, as if he knew he had said enough, he turned back to his lunch.

CHAPTER FIVE

When Conor hadn't rung again by seven o'clock that evening, Olivia decided to ring him.

It wasn't the wisest thing to do. She knew that. Stephen's arrival hadn't made her feelings for Conor any easier to understand, but at least her ex-husband's presence did provide what she was doing with a little justification. She needed someone to talk to, and there wasn't anybody else.

Not that she intended to discuss Stephen with Conor, she reflected dourly. Although he was now occupying the room across the hall from her own, she was determined to ignore the fact. No, she needed someone to talk to who wasn't Stephen, and who didn't know Stephen. Someone who wouldn't tell her she was crazy for allowing him to stay at the inn.

She sighed. She was a fool for allowing him to do so, nevertheless. She knew that, too. She didn't owe Stephen a thing, and his present predicament was no more than he deserved. His story—that Karen Darcy had pursued him both at and after the Christmas party, and not the other way around—was hardly credible, but, either way, if Harry Darcy found out, the result was likely to be the same. Stephen's boss was known to be insanely jealous of his young wife, and any suspicion that one of his employees might be involved with her could cause untold repercussions. To say that Stephen would immediately find himself without a job was the least of it. Olivia knew Harry Darcy, and her opinion was that he would not be content with simply sacking the culprit. In his own world, Harry was a powerful man, and the possibilities of how he might take his revenge were endless.

Which was the prime reason she had agreed to help Stephen, Olivia realised now. In spite of his threats, she felt sorry for him, and she had no wish to play any part in his downfall. If, by pretending she and Stephen were still on friendly terms, if, by saying, should she be asked, that he had spent a particular evening with her, and not with Karen, she could divert Harry's wrath, she would do it. She didn't like it. But she liked the thought of the possible consequences of not doing so even less.

Now, after pressing the button to obtain an outside line, she dialled the number she had found in the local directory. It had been listed under Conor's name only, with no mention of Sharon or his medical status.

Listening to it ring, Olivia contemplated what she would say if Sharon answered. She ought to have something prepared, something more than just an urgent need to hear a friendly voice. Sharon already thought she was a nuisance. How would she regard an unsolicited phone call?

Well, it wasn't entirely unsolicited, Olivia defended herself swiftly. Conor had rung her that morning. She was only returning his call. Yes, she decided, that was how she would phrase it, if Sharon answered. She had waited until the evening to ring, because she had assumed Conor would be spending the day at the clinic.

All the same, her palm was slick as it gripped the phone, and when, after three rings, the call was connected, she almost rang off. But, as she hesitated, there was a click, and Conor's recorded voice came on the line to inform her that he was unavailable at that moment. The message went on to say she should leave her name and number, and the time of her call, and he'd get back to her.

Dammit! Olivia sighed in frustration. She hated talking to a machine. And what she hated even more was the thought that Sharon might be the one to listen to her message. She was tempted not to leave one.

The recorded voice had finished and the bleep advising her to say her piece had sounded. If she was going to answer, now was the time to do it. Or did she want Conor to think there was some pervert on the line?

Expelling her breath rather quickly, she hurried into speech. 'Conor, um—this is Olivia——'

'Liv!' Conor's instant response had her sucking in her breath again in sharp surprise. 'Live, are you still there? Sorry about this, but I was in the shower. I heard the phone ringing, but it took me a couple of minutes to grab a towel.'

'Oh.'

Olivia couldn't think of anything else to say at that moment, and he went on, 'I was going to ring you later. Didn't you get my message this morning?'

'Well—yes.' Olivia realised how pathetic she must sound, admitting she had been too eager to speak to him to wait for his call. 'It was just that——' she sought desperately for an excuse '—well, that I'm going to have dinner, and I didn't want you to ring when—when I wasn't here.'

'You're having dinner *now*?' Conor sounded impatient. 'Liv, it's only seven o'clock!'

'I know that.' Olivia could hear the impatience in her tone now, but it was just a defence against the disbelief she could hear in his. 'Anyway, I—I just wanted to take the opportunity to thank you again for taking pity on me last night. It was good of you and—and Sharon— to let me share your evening. I'm sure I cramped your style, and I want you to know I appreciate the trouble you——'

'What trouble?' Conor cut into her pitiable monologue to voice his own frustration, and Olivia wondered fleetingly if Sharon was listening to what they were saying. 'For Christ's sake, Liv, stop talking as if what I did was an act of charity or something. I wanted to spend the evening with you, for God's sake! I was hoping you'd let me do the same tonight.'

Olivia swallowed. 'Tonight?' she echoed faintly.

'Yes, tonight.' He sighed. 'Look, I suppose I should have rung earlier, but things have been pretty hectic today. We had an emergency at the clinic, and I didn't get away until after six. Then, when I got home, I went straight into the shower. But my intention was to get dressed and come down to see you. I guess I thought you'd find it harder to turn me down if we were face to face.'

Olivia's tongue circled her dry lips. 'I see.' But she didn't really. Was he asking her to spend another evening with himself and Sharon?

'I thought you might be agreeable to me fetching you back here,' he appended, adding to her confusion. His voice took on a persuasive note. 'We could have a pizza out of the freezer, or I have been known to produce a fairly decent omelette. What d'you say?'

Olivia shook her head. 'I—don't know——'

'What don't you know?' Conor sounded impatient again. 'Damn, I knew I should have come to see you myself.' He paused. 'Look, give me five minutes to put on some clothes, and I'll come down to the harbour. I won't be long, and you can tell me what you want to do over a half of lager——'

'No!'

'Liv——'

'I mean...' Olivia decided that anything was better than spending the evening dodging her ex-husband. 'I— I will have dinner with you. But I'll meet you outside in—in twenty minutes?'

'Make that fifteen,' amended Conor roughly, and, without giving her a chance to argue, he rang off.

Of course, as soon as he had done so, Olivia's doubts returned. It was all very well wanting to evade Stephen's company, but was spending another evening with Conor a sensible alternative? After what had happened the night before, she ought to be avoiding anything that might aggravate her awareness of him, and what would Mrs

Drake think if she found out that Mrs Perry was going out without her husband?

Deciding it was too late now to be having such thoughts, Olivia surveyed the clothes she had brought with her with critical eyes. She couldn't wear the same dress she had worn the night before, and if they were eating at home something more casual was obviously called for. The trouble was that clothes had not figured high on her agenda when she decided she needed to get away. In consequence, she had filled her suitcase with the first warm items that had come to hand, and she realised now how limited she was.

The ski pants she had worn the morning she walked up to Gull Rise seemed the most attractive. Black, and narrow-fitting, they clung to her slim hips like a second skin. But at least she had no unsightly bulges, she thought wryly. Even if she knew she could have done with a few more pounds of flesh on her bones.

Another chunky sweater completed the outfit: a creamy Aran knit, whose wide neckline tended to slip off her shoulder. It was just as well she didn't need to wear a bra, she thought. She certainly hadn't thought to pack a strapless one.

Sitting at the dressing-table a few moments later, trying to find some more attractive way to do her hair, a wave of self-disgust swept over her. What was she doing? she asked herself, dragging the coarse curls back into their usual knot. Conor already knew what she looked like. There was no point in trying to look younger than she was. Sharon would know immediately what she was doing, and did she really want to lose the slight advantage that being older gave her?

She was putting on her coat when someone knocked at her door. Conor? she wondered, her heart racing, but when she called, 'Yes?' it wasn't Conor's voice that answered.

'Ollie!' Stephen's irritating abbreviation of her name came clearly through the panels, and she was inordinately glad she had locked the door earlier. 'Ollie, are you ready? I thought we might go down and have a drink before dinner.'

Olivia caught her breath. Just like that, she mused incredulously. He really thought they could behave as if nothing had happened. A drink; dinner. My God, she wouldn't be surprised if he was considering asking her to spend the night with him! Why not? she reflected cynically. Sleeping with a woman didn't mean that much to Stephen. He had done it often enough, goodness knows!

'I...' Her hands tortured the lapels of her coat, as she fought back the urge to tell him what he could do with his invitation. 'Well——' she licked her lips '—I'm not ready yet, Stephen. Why—why don't you just go ahead? I'll—see you later.' And so she would. Though perhaps later than Stephen imagined.

'OK.' Clearly the prospect of another pint of Tom Drake's lager was attractive enough to save any argument. 'I'll be in the bar.'

'Fine.'

Olivia was amazed he couldn't hear the sound of her heart beating. It seemed to be pounding in her chest. But, happily, her ex-husband had no reason to assume that she meant anything other than his interpretation of her words, and she heard the creak of the banister as he started down the stairs.

Only then did she expel her breath on a long sigh. Dear lord, she breathed, and she had left London to avoid any more stress! Now she had the problem of getting out of the inn without either Stephen or the Drakes observing her departure.

In the event, it was easier than she had anticipated. There were already several customers, as well as Stephen, in the bar, and at this hour of the evening Mrs Drake was, as usual, busy in the kitchen. The inn supplied a modest selection of bar meals, as well as those that were served in the dining-room, and, although many of them were of the instant variety, Mrs Drake liked to supervise

their preparation. No doubt she was preparing something special to celebration her husband's arrival, reflected Olivia ruefully. Well, Stephen would enjoy it
anyway. She just hoped he didn't see her absence as an
excuse to pump the landlady about her possible
whereabouts.

It was raining outside, but at least it wasn't as cold as
it had been the previous evening. Nevertheless, Olivia
hoped she wouldn't have to wait long before Conor got
there. Even with her coat collar tipped high about her
ears, she felt a drop of dampness invading her neck.

When a car skidded to a halt beside her, she drew
back in some alarm. But then, recognising the muddy
Audi, she stepped forward again, barely avoiding the
passenger door, which was thrust open savagely from
inside.

'What the hell are you doing, standing in the rain?'
snarled Conor, as she got awkwardly into the seat beside
him. 'God, when you said you'd meet me outside, I
didn't realise you meant it literally!'

Olivia sucked in her breath. 'I don't think there's any
need to be so rude, Conor. I'm here, aren't I? You didn't
have to wait for me, as I've had to do for you. You said
fifteen minutes. You should have stuck to the twenty as
I suggested.'

Conor's face was grim as he slammed the car into gear
and took off again as aggressively as he had arrived.
'Don't patronise me, Liv,' he retorted, as she hastily
groped for the seatbelt. 'What's the matter? Having
second thoughts?'

Olivia gasped. She'd had just about enough of being
made to feel as if she had something to be guilty about,
first with Stephen, and now with Conor. 'It seems to me
that you're the one having second thoughts,' she returned coldly. 'But don't worry about it. You can always
take me back.'

'Don't talk rubbish!' In the subdued light from the dashboard, she saw his face take on an exasperated expression. 'Just because I was concerned about you!'

'Oh!' Olivia jammed the safety clip into place. 'Is that what it was? You could have fooled me.'

Conor gave her a fulminating look. 'Will you stop trying to turn this into something it's not? I was annoyed, that's all. Did you have to make your reluctance to be seen with me so obvious?'

Olivia shook her head. 'That—that's stupid!'

'Is it?' Conor arched one brow. 'So why did you want to meet me outside?'

'I—had my reasons.'

'What reasons?'

Olivia sighed. 'Look, does it matter? You'll just have to believe me when I say it had nothing to do with—with who you are. It's not as if the Drakes don't know we know one another. Heavens, Mrs Drake was telling me how she went to school with Sharon's mother.'

'Really?' Conor's brows descended. 'I got the impression you kept yourself pretty much to yourself. I wouldn't have thought you were the type to enjoy a heart-to-heart with old Eva!'

'Old Eva? Oh, you mean Mrs Drake.' Olivia stiffened her shoulders. 'Well, that's what we old women do, didn't you know? Gossip about the past!'

'You're not an old woman,' replied Conor irritably. 'God, what are you trying to do here, Liv? Ruin the evening before it's begun?'

'I think you did that already,' she retorted heatedly, and the expletive he uttered successfully silenced her for the remainder of the journey.

Consequently, when they turned into the gates of Conor's house, Olivia was already searching for reasons why she shouldn't stay long. Perhaps she could pretend her leg was hurting her, she considered. It was a sufficiently ambiguous statement not to require too much elaboration. Indeed, she wondered now why she hadn't just used it as an excuse earlier. She could always have asked Mrs Drake to serve her dinner in her room, thus saving herself from Stephen's company, too.

The car had stopped, she realised suddenly, and while she had been musing over what she might have done Conor had got out and come round to open her door. 'Come on,' he said. 'If *you* don't mind getting soaked, *I* do.'

It was hardly gracious, but she allowed him to take her gloved hand and help her to her feet. After all, if she wanted to foster the belief that her leg was giving her trouble, it wouldn't do to be too independent.

'Thank you,' she said politely, as he leant forward to slam the door behind her, and his lean tanned features softened into a rueful grin.

'I'm sorry,' he said huskily, rubbing the knuckles of one hand down her cheek. 'I guess you think I'm a bastard, mmm?'

Olivia's throat constricted. 'I—I—*no*! No, of course not.' It was an effort to keep her tone impersonal. 'Don't be silly, Conor.'

His hand fell away. 'If you persist in treating me like a schoolboy, I may be forced to prove you wrong,' he answered, turning away to climb the steps and insert his key in the lock. He glanced back. 'Are you coming, or do you need some help?'

'I can do it.'

Olivia used the iron handrail to mount the steps behind him, surprised that Sharon hadn't come out to see what was taking them so long. There were lights on in the house, and because the curtains were not yet drawn she could see into the elegant drawing-room. Someone had lit a fire, and it was burning cosily in the grate. It gave the room such a familiar look that she wouldn't have been surprised to see Conor's parents sitting on the sofa. For a moment, the thought of how things might have been filled her with regret. No wonder Conor had wanted to keep the house. It must be filled with memories.

Conor thrust the door open, and the light from inside spilled on to Olivia's pale face. 'Now, what is it?' he demanded, glimpsing something of the sadness she was feeling, and Olivia shook her head.

'I was just thinking about your mother and father,' she admitted unwillingly, following him into the hall. 'I understand now why you wanted to keep the house.'

'Do you?'

Conor's response was vaguely enigmatic, and Olivia turned to close the door. Then, tugging off her gloves, she thrust them into her pockets, before tackling the buttons on her coat. But every minute she expected Sharon to come bursting out to meet them, eager to demonstrate her authority as mistress of the house. Even if it was in name only, thought Olivia, rather maliciously. Though she knew that, if Sharon had her way, that would only be a matter of time.

She was easing the coat off her shoulders when Conor seemed to remember his manners, and came to help her. His cool fingers brushed the nape of her neck as he did so, and she shivered. It was too easy to imagine how those hard fingers would feel touching her with more than just accidental intent, and she drew an uneven breath as he hung the coat on the old-fashioned umbrella stand.

'Go ahead,' he said, as she waited uncertainly for him to finish. 'You know the way.'

'Into the drawing-room?' she ventured, unwilling, in spite of everything, to steal Sharon's thunder.

'Sure.' Conor was removing the leather jacket he had worn to fetch her, revealing a black shirt and black jeans. He came up behind her, and the heat from his body was palpably real. 'What are you waiting for?'

'I—um...' Olivia moved hurriedly away from him. 'Wh—where's Sharon?'

'Sharon?' Conor's astonishment was not feigned. 'Did I give you any reason to think she would be here?'

'Er—no.' Olivia stepped somewhat nervously into the drawing-room. 'But—well, where is she? She hasn't gone out for the evening because she knew I was coming, has she?'

Conor gave her an old-fashioned look. 'Why do I get the feeling we're talking at cross purposes here?' he asked wryly. 'Let me get this straight—Sharon told you she lived here, right?'

Olivia gripped the back of a Regency-striped armchair. 'No-o.'

'Did I?'

She shook her head. 'No.'

'OK.' He inclined his head and started across the room to where a tray of drinks was residing on a low bookcase. 'I'm glad we've cleared that up. So—what are you going to have to drink? I've got scotch and sherry, and sherry and scotch.' He grimaced. 'I was going to buy a bottle of gin, when I came down to the pub. But—well, it didn't work out that way, did it?'

Olivia caught her lower lip between her teeth. 'Sharon doesn't live here?' she asked, still not quite able to believe it, and Conor unscrewed the cap of the sherry and filled two glasses.

'No,' he replied patiently, and, lifting both glasses, he carried them towards her. 'Here. I'm assuming you're not opposed to an appetiser.' He handed one of the glasses to her, and she wondered if he noticed her scramble to grasp the stem to avoid his fingers. 'Cheers.'

'Cheers,' she echoed faintly, taking a sip of the dry sack. 'Mmm—this is nice.'

'Is it?' Conor's mouth compressed. 'So, what made you think Sharon lived here?' he probed. 'Did Mrs Drake tell you that?'

'No.' Olivia shifted a little uncomfortably. 'I—I've obviously made a mistake.'

'In coming here?' enquired Conor drily. He gestured towards the sofa. 'Why don't we sit down? Then you can tell me all about it. Right now, I get the feeling that one wrong word from me and you'll be dashing to phone a cab!'

'That's silly.' Olivia expelled her breath rather unevenly.

'So?' Conor bent to switch on another lamp. 'I don't bite, you know. Well,' he grinned, as he straightened, 'only occasionally.'

Clutching her glass, Olivia circled the armchair, and went to perch on the end of the sofa. She would have preferred to sit in the armchair, but she had already aroused his amusement, and she had no wish to make a complete laughing-stock of herself. Besides, it was warmer on the sofa.

She had stretched out her toes toward the blaze, when Conor came to sit beside her. Unlike her, he didn't balance on the edge of the seat, but dropped heavily on to the cushions, his long black-clad legs only inches from hers.

'Comfortable, isn't it?' he remarked, crossing his feet at the ankle. 'You've no idea how often I longed to experience a real winter again, when I was living in Florida.'

Olivia relaxed a little. 'Don't they have winters in Florida?'

Conor tipped his head back against the cushions. 'Oh, yeah,' he said cynically, 'they have winters. Maybe once in ten, twenty years the temperature drops below freezing, and all the growers panic in case it kills the fruit trees. I believe they even had snow, once. But I didn't see it. Where we lived, on the Gulf coast, it rarely drops below sixty. That's Fahrenheit, of course.'

Olivia was impressed. 'I'd say there are quite a few people who'd envy you, living in a semi-tropical climate like that,' she said. She took another sip of her sherry. 'I almost envy you myself.'

'So why didn't you go somewhere warm to recuperate?' Conor's eyes were intent. 'Instead of coming here.'

'Oh...' Olivia shrugged. 'I didn't want to go where there were lots of people. I wanted some peace and quiet. And you have to admit, Paget has that.'

'But without your husband,' murmured Conor quietly, and she was glad she could blame the fire for her hot face.

'Stephen has a job to do,' she replied obliquely, wondering how long it would be before he found out that her ex-husband had spent a night at the inn. 'Um—tell me about your job at the clinic. Is it like a hospital? Are the people sick, or what?'

'Oh, yes. They're sick.' Conor let himself be diverted, and to her relief his gaze turned to the fire. 'But it's not really like a hospital. More like a prison, I guess.'

'Go on.'

Olivia was intrigued, and Conor good-naturedly explained a little about its purpose. 'We deal with a lot of habitual offenders. The kind you've probably defended in court. Addicts who, for one reason or another, can't— or won't—kick the habit.'

'Young people?'

'Addicts tend to be young,' remarked Conor drily. 'Not a lot of them make it into old age.'

'But—I mean—juvenile offenders.'

'No. Mostly they're late teens or twenties. But I'm talking about real people here. Young men and women from all walks of life. Not just the pimps and the pushers.'

'And you counsel them?'

Conor pulled a face. 'Well, we try to. David Marshall—he's the guy who runs the place—he's working on the theory that people have to *want* to be cured before it happens.'

'So what causes young people to turn to drugs? Curiosity? Peer pressure?'

'It's not as simple as that. The theory that kids take to drugs because their friends are doing it doesn't really hold up. If that were true, or if it only worked that way, all young people would be potential addicts. But they're not.' He paused. 'That's not to say that most young people aren't exposed to drugs at some time in their life. They are. The widespread use of heroin and cocaine is a very real problem. Teachers find needles behind the bike sheds these days, as they used to find condoms years ago.' He gave a rueful grin. 'Unfortunately, these days they find both.'

Olivia's lips twitched. 'So what's your theory?'

'It's a lot of things. I think television has a lot to answer for.'

'The violence, you mean?'

'Not in this case, no.' Conor shook his head. 'Oh, I'm sure the amount of violence we all see on television has some bearing on the way we live our lives. There's no doubt that it's a powerful force for change. And kids are brainwashed to the extent that when they see real pictures of dead bodies it doesn't mean anything. I read a report once about some teenagers being shown a video that was shot in Vietnam. The pictures were horrific, really gruesome, but they didn't turn a hair. It was the guy teaching them who threw his guts up in the john.'

'What did you mean, then?'

'Oh—aspirations, I guess.' Conor spoke flatly. 'Television makes people feel inadequate. Particularly young people. They see people living in glossy houses, driving glossy cars and living glossy lives, while they can't even get a job. What do you think that does to them?'

'But they're not *real* people,' exclaimed Olivia, and Conor gave her a narrow-eyed stare.

'But they are,' he declared softly. 'To some of the kids I deal with, they're just as real as the old lady who got mugged in her armchair, or the napalm victims in Vietnam.'

Olivia swallowed. 'So what can we do?'

'Is that a rhetorical question, or do you mean what can *I* do?'

Olivia looked rueful. 'Both, I suppose.'

'Well...' Conor slid the fingers of one hand through his hair until they came to rest at the back of his neck. 'I guess I have to try and convince them that there's more to life than what they see on television.'

'And do you succeed?'

'Who knows?' Conor's hand dropped to his chest, drawing her unwilling attention to the fine pale hair nestling in the opened V of his shirt. 'We seem to. But it's not possible to keep track of what happens to all of them after they leave the clinic.'

Olivia nodded. 'And what kind of treatment do they get?'

'After we've got them off the hard drugs, you mean?' He shrugged. 'Well, in addition to the counselling, there's therapy; sometimes psychotherapy, although that doesn't work for everyone.'

'So what do you do then?'

Conor's lips twisted. 'Hey, that's enough about what I do.' He surveyed her with wry amusement, and then lifted his hand to squeeze the back of her neck. 'I don't want to spend the whole evening talking about me.'

Olivia quivered. His fingers were absurdly intimate, and although she had expected him to let go of her again he didn't. He just sat looking at her with that disturbingly sensual green gaze, and she was helpless against the insidious emotions he aroused inside her.

CHAPTER SIX

'OH—I'M not very interesting,' she denied now, and the jerky movement she made had the neckline of the sweater sliding off one soft shoulder.

'I disagree.' Conor's eyes darkened as they fastened on that vulnerable exposure of flesh, and his hand slid from her nape to her shoulder. 'It's like silk,' he said, almost to himself, his eyes dropping to follow the caressing movement of his brown fingers against her pale skin. 'But you're too thin. What have you been doing to yourself?'

'I—I thought thin was supposed to be fashionable,' Olivia protested lightly, and, gathering her scattered senses, she got abruptly to her feet. 'Um—what was that you said about an omelette? I'm hungry.'

She wasn't, of course, and she was sure Conor knew it. But he swallowed the remainder of the sherry in his glass, and obediently stood up. 'You can choose,' he said, matching his tone to hers. 'I found some ribs in the freezer, as well as the pizza. Come and see.'

She let him lead the way into the kitchen, which was at the back of the house. The dark oak units and terracotta tiles had been Sally's pride and joy, and Olivia had lost count of the number of meals the four of them had eaten at the stripped-pine table.

It was dark, and when Conor switched on the lights they illuminated the pile of unwashed dishes in the sink. 'Unfortunately, Mum didn't see any need for a dishwasher,' he remarked, steering her away from them. 'Just ignore the mess. I'll clear up later.'

'I'll do them,' declared Olivia firmly, grateful to have something uncontroversial to do. 'Shall I make the omelettes, too?'

'No.' Conor gave her an aggrieved look. 'I'm not one of those guys who can't even boil an egg. I've had to look after myself for quite some time now, and, as you can see, I haven't starved.'

'That's the truth,' murmured Olivia barely audibly, but he heard her.

'So?' he challenged. 'Is there something wrong with the way I look?'

'No, of course not.' Olivia was glad she could busy herself running water into the sink. But she couldn't help thinking that Conor would probably be shocked if he knew what she had been thinking about his lean, muscled frame. His touching her might have been quite innocent, but her thoughts at this moment were definitely not. And it disturbed her.

'How about if we have a pizza omelette?' he suggested, opening the freezer door, and Olivia lifted her head to see him watching her reflection in the darkened glass of the window.

'A pizza omelette?' she echoed faintly. 'Can you have such a thing?'

'Hey, when I was in med. school, I ate anything going,' he responded, grinning. 'But OK. Maybe a pizza omelette isn't such a good idea. How about pizza *and* omelette, with a little green salad to satisfy the health nuts?'

Olivia laughed. She couldn't help herself. And, as she did so, she realised how long it was since she had had so much fun. Even with her hands plunged in soapy water, and a pile of dishes waiting to be dried beside her, she was enjoying herself. Being with Conor was like being young again. She had forgotten what it was like to be foolish and carefree.

'That sounds good,' said Conor, suddenly behind her, his reflection looming above her in the now misty glass. His hands descended on her shoulders for a moment, before sliding down her arms and away. 'You should laugh more often. I like it.'

Somehow, Olivia managed to get the remainder of the dishes washed and dried, and by the time she had done so the pizza was hissing in the microwave, and the omelettes were bubbling in the pan.

They ate, as Olivia remembered them doing so many times before, at the kitchen table. Conor had half-heartedly offered to lay the table in the dining-room, but Olivia had been adamant.

'It's nicer in here,' she said. 'Cosier.' And then looked away from his lazy gaze, with a feeling almost of panic. She was enjoying this too much, she thought unsteadily. Just because Sharon wasn't here, that didn't mean she didn't exist.

Nevertheless, she ate the food Conor had prepared with more enthusiasm than she had felt for years. The pizza, oozing with cheese, made a remarkably delicious accompaniment to the omelettes, and the crisp salad was served with a yoghurt dressing that was tart and refreshing. There was even warm French bread and butter, had she wanted it, but although she enjoyed watching Conor munching through its golden crust she couldn't manage anything else.

'Good?' he enquired, when they were both reduced to sipping glasses of the smooth hock he had supplied with the food, and Olivia nodded.

'Very good,' she agreed, stroking the film of condensation that had settled on her glass. 'I feel pleasantly full, and——'

'—mellow,' put in Conor softly, pushing back his chair, and getting up. 'Let's go and finish the wine in the other room.'

'But what about clearing up?' protested Olivia, looking up at him, and his lips twisted.

'Not right now,' he stated, coming round the table to draw back her chair. 'Come on. It's happy hour.'

Conor drew the curtains across the drawing-room windows, immediately reducing the dimensions of the room to the lamplit area by the fire. Then, after waiting until Olivia had seated herself on the sofa again, he tossed another log on the glowing coals and resumed his place beside her.

'OK,' he said quietly, 'are you going to tell me why you thought I lived with Sharon?' He sighed. 'And sit back, can't you? I want to look at you, not your back!'

Olivia could have told him that that was exactly why she was sitting perched on the edge of the cushions, but she didn't. Easing her hips a little way further on to the seat, she gave an uncertain shrug. 'I thought I did. Tell you why I thought you lived with Sharon, I mean.'

'No.' To her alarm, Conor's hand descended on her shoulder again, but all he did was urge her against the cushions at her back. 'You said you'd made a mistake. I'm curious to know why.'

'Oh, come on.' Thankfully, he had released her as soon as he achieved his objective, and she realised her best option was to attack his argument. 'That morning, when I walked up here, well—you're not going to tell me she hadn't spent the night here——'

Conor arched a quizzical brow. 'Why not?'

'Why not?' Olivia hadn't thought he would contradict her. 'Well, because—because——'

'As a matter of fact, she'd called in on her way to work,' he essayed flatly. And then, meeting Olivia's disbelieving gaze, he added, 'I'm not saying she hasn't slept here. She has. I'm not a saint, Liv. I need sexual satisfaction, just like anyone else.' His eyes darkened. 'As you do.'

That was a little close to the bone, and Olivia hurriedly transferred her attention back to her wine. 'Even so——'

'Even so—what?' Conor leaned forward so that he could look into her face. 'Sharon was acting as if she owned me, is that what you're trying to say?'

Olivia stifled the gulp of panic that was rising in her throat. 'It—it's nothing to do with me.'

'Isn't it?' Conor's voice was incredibly soft. 'You're not interested in what I do with Sharon, is that right?'

'Conor.' Olivia moistened her dry lips, and somehow managed to meet his probing gaze. 'Don't you think this is a rather pointless conversation? You have your life to lead. And—and I have mine. Did—er—did I tell you I'd been offered a partnership with—with Hallidays?'

'It doesn't surprise me.' Conor shrugged. 'You always were ambitious.'

Olivia was taken aback. 'Do you think so?'

'I know so.' Conor's voice was dry as he leant forward to put his empty glass on the coffee-table.

'How?'

He lounged back beside her. 'You don't have any family, do you?'

'Children, you mean?'

'What else?'

Olivia tried to gather her composure. 'Isn't that a rather sexist remark?'

'All remarks are sexist, I guess.'

'No, you know what I mean.'

'Why? Because it challenges your femininity?'

Olivia straightened her spine. 'How do you know I haven't tried to have children?'

'Have you?'

Olivia gasped. 'That's my business.' She used the excuse of putting down her glass to evade his enquiring stare. Then, running a nervous hand over the knot at her nape, she took a surreptitious look at her watch. 'Heavens, is that the time?'

'It's only nine-thirty,' he remarked mildly. And, before she could say anything more, his hand curled around her neck, under her hair. 'You're not going yet.'

She'd never expected him to restrain her; not like that: so proprietorially, so *possessively*. As if he thought he had the right to keep her there against her will, she thought unsteadily. His hard fingers moved sinuously against her flesh, and her heart palpitated wildly. Dear

God, what was he doing? And why was she letting him do it?

'Conor!' Her protest was strangled, but then, putting on her coolest, most authoritative voice, she added, 'Don't do that!'

'Don't do what?' he asked softly, moving closer, and if she had had any doubts that she was over-reacting they were quickly dispelled. His warm, wine-scented breath caressed her cheek. 'Oh, Liv,' he breathed, 'you have no idea what I want to do.'

Common sense wasn't working. 'Conor,' she exclaimed again, and this time she tried to lighten her tone. 'Conor, I think you're teasing me. Now, come on. Let me go.'

But that didn't work either. Instead, she felt the pins that held her hair in place being deliberately withdrawn, and, although she put up her hands to stop him, presently the unruly cloud of dark hair tumbled about her shoulders.

'Mmm. That's better,' he said, ignoring her astounded expression, and, taking a handful of hair, he threaded it through his fingers. 'I've been wanting to do this ever since you got here.'

'And now you have,' said Olivia tautly, letting him see how angry he had made her. 'Conor, I don't know what you think you're doing, but I think this has gone far enough. Now, I suggest you call me a cab——'

'It hasn't,' he cut in huskily, still smoothing her hair between his fingers, and her dark brows drew together.

'What are you talking——?'

'Gone far enough,' he appended huskily, drawing the neckline of her sweater aside, and touching her shoulder with his tongue. 'I haven't gone nearly far enough.'

Olivia jerked her shoulder away from his mouth. 'Conor, what on earth do you think I am?'

His eyes lifted to hers. 'I think you're a beautiful woman,' he replied simply, and she gasped.

'I think you've taken leave of your senses,' she retorted, grimly hanging on to her sanity. 'Conor, you're not a boy any more!'

'Would you let me do this if I were?'

'No!' Olivia felt as if she was getting into deeper and deeper water. 'Conor, I'm married!' she declared, using her erstwhile status as a final attempt to deter him, and then shrank back in alarm when his hand came to cup her face.

'D'you think I don't know that?' he demanded, his thumb and forefinger digging into her cheeks. His eyes moved almost hungrily over her shocked features for a moment, and then softened.

'Anyway, what's wrong with me wanting to kiss you? You never used to object before.'

Olivia's senses felt scrambled. 'You—you know what's wrong,' she got out jerkily. 'As—as I said, you're not a boy now. And—and I don't appreciate being put in this position.'

'What position?' His thumb brushed her mouth, and, almost against her will, her lips parted against that sensuous abrasion. The pad of his thumb probed inside her mouth, scraping the tender flesh inside her lower lip, and smearing its wetness against her chin. 'How many positions do you know?'

Olivia caught her breath. 'Conor...' she began again, but, before she could voice her faltering indignation, his lips took the place of his thumb.

Pure, unadulterated panic gripped her now. As his warm mouth brushed lightly over hers, and the hand that had been holding her face in place slid caressingly to her throat, the recklessness of what she was doing swept over her. But she wasn't afraid of Conor. It wasn't fear of him that was turning her limbs to water. It was the clear and certain knowledge that she wanted him to kiss her just as much as he wanted to do it.

'Sweet,' he muttered roughly, his mouth settling more firmly over hers, and the hot invasion of his tongue was like a shaft of electricity jolting through her. It plunged deeply into her mouth, filling her with the feel and the taste of him, seductive, and velvety, and achingly real.

Olivia moaned in protest, but it was a puny thing at best, and the hands that had balled against his flat midriff opened like the petals of a flower against his chest. But they didn't keep him away from her. On the contrary; when she felt the thudding beat of his heart beneath her hands, she shuddered uncontrollably, and she clutched handfuls of his shirt with fingers that were damp and greedy. God, she trembled, with her last coherent thought, what was he doing to her?

Her head sank into the cushions behind her, and Conor's fingers slid along her hot cheek, holding her a prisoner beneath his hungry mouth. And that mouth strayed from her lips to her eyes, closing her lids with feathery light kisses, so that her world was reduced to one of touching, and feeling, and shattering sensation. He kissed the curve of her cheekbones, the dark arch of her eyebrows. His tongue explored the unexpectedly sensitive cavern of her ear, and his teeth fastened on her earlobe, though the pain was not unpleasurable. On the contrary, Olivia was discovering that hitherto unknown areas of her face and neck were incredibly responsive to his touch, and each new invasion caused the tight pain of awareness to stir deep inside her.

The blood was pounding in her head, but it was thick and turgid, battling through her veins in an effort to bring oxygen to her swimming senses. She felt as if she were drowning in emotion, and, totally against her will, her hands groped for his neck. Her fingers tangled in the silky hair at his nape, and she clung to him helplessly, caught in a spell that was older than time itself.

Conor's breathing had quickened, too, and when he sought her lips again there was urgency as well as pulsing passion in the demanding pressure of his mouth. She felt his hand invade the neckline of her sweater, smoothing the fine bones of her shoulders, before attempting to reach her throbbing breasts. But the neckline wasn't loose enough for that, and his hand slid down to find the button-hard nipples, taut beneath the rough wool of the sweater. He rolled the sensitive little peak against his palm, and Olivia couldn't suppress the gulp of anguish she felt at the harsh abrasion. And, as if sensing her discomfort, Conor's hand moved down to the hem of her sweater, slipping beneath the wool to find the soft flesh beneath. His hands caressed her slim waist, one finger probing the buttoned fastening of her trousers, before moving up again to take possession of one swollen breast.

'Better?' he breathed against her mouth, and she felt herself nodding, mindlessly. In her present state of responsiveness, he could have stripped the clothes from her and she wouldn't have objected. She was completely caught up in the things he was doing to her body, and the fact that he was becoming as sexually aroused in the process as she was didn't really register.

She had slipped lower on the sofa, and Conor was lying half over her now. When he moved to wedge one leg between hers, her legs splayed automatically. It made it easier to accommodate the disturbing ache she could feel between her legs, and when he rubbed his thigh against that throbbing juncture she made a convulsive little sound of pleasure, and moved against him.

'God, Liv!' he choked, and it was the words he spoke that made her aware that he was trembling. Made her aware, too, of the thrusting pressure of his manhood, throbbing against her thigh, threatening to split the zip of his trousers. 'Let me make love with you.'

And, although the blinding instincts of desire urged her to go on, to reach down and open his zip, and let him do what he wanted, the cool breath of reality was rearing its ugly head. What was she doing? she asked herself in dismay. How had she allowed such a situation to develop?

The awareness of her own complicity caused a wave of embarrassment to envelop her. Dear lord, she thought, it wasn't as if she were a naïve girl, unaware of what happened when a woman allowed a man to kiss her, and caress her, and touch her naked breasts. Indeed, she doubted anyone was that naïve these days. And particularly not a woman who had been married and divorced, and whose husband had proved so susceptible to the temptations of the flesh. Dammit, there were no excuses for what she was doing, even if, for a short time, he had caused her to abandon her identity. And that had never happened before.

She shifted beneath him then, pushing his leg away from that most sensitive part of her anatomy, and struggling to ease herself up against the cushions. God, had she really let *Conor* do this to her? She must have drunk more wine that she'd realised. There could be no other reason for her behaviour.

'Hey—Liv!' Conor's reaction to her withdrawal was not unexpectedly impatient. 'Don't do that,' he protested, when she put both hands against his chin and tried to push him away. 'What are you trying to do? Break my neck?'

Olivia fought back a sob. 'Let me up, Conor,' she exclaimed, not answering him. 'For God's sake, let go of me!'

'What's wrong?' Resisting her efforts to force him away from her, Conor looked down at her with anxious eyes. 'Did I hurt you or something? Talk to me, dammit. What did I do?'

Olivia caught her breath. 'What didn't you do?' she cried, bringing a look of dawning comprehension to those sea-green eyes. 'Conor, get off me! I want to get up.'

Conor's long lashes veiled his eyes. He could still see her, but she didn't find it so easy to read his expression any more. 'Don't you think you're over-reacting?' he suggested softly, but there was a thread of exasperation in his voice now, and she told herself she was glad.

'Possibly,' she responded, wishing she had more experience in these matters. She had the feeling she was handling this badly, but she didn't know what else to do. 'Look,' she added, 'as I'm quite a lot older than you are, you'll just have to take my word that this was a mistake. Trust me. It was.'

Conor watched her tugging her sweater down over her hips, and then said evenly, 'Not that much older,' and she realised it was going to be even harder than she'd thought.

'I was your mother's friend,' she pointed out tensely, aware that her body was not responding to the dictates of her brain. 'How—how do you think she would feel, if she could see us now?'

Conor shrugged. Clearly that consequence didn't bother him. 'You're not old enough to be my mother,' was all he said. And then, huskily, 'I got the distinct impression that you didn't exactly object to what I was doing.'

'Well, you were wrong!' Olivia swallowed on the lie, and resumed her efforts to shift him. 'I was a fool to come here. I should have stuck to my original intention, and refused your invitation.'

Conor's mouth thinned. 'That was your original intention? To turn me down?'

'Yes.' That, at least, was true.

'Why?'

'Why?' Olivia took an uneven breath. 'I just told you why.'

'No. You've just spun me a tale about your being too old for me.' One brow arched. 'That's bullshit!'

'Conor, I mean it——'

'So do I.' And, avoiding her fluttering hands, he pushed his fingers into the coarse tangle of black curls that framed her flushed face. Then, bending his head, he brushed her quivering mouth with his, and a helpless shiver of anticipation enveloped her. 'You have no idea how long I've wanted to have you like this,' he told her roughly. 'God, I used to fantasise about how you'd look—how you'd feel.' His lips twisted. 'So don't expect me to react favourably when you tell me this is all a mistake. Don't expect me to believe it either.'

'Even if it's true?'

'I don't believe you.' Conor was infuriatingly complacent. 'And before you hit me with the fact that you're married, and that I shouldn't be lusting after a married woman, I want to say I don't think much of a man who abandons his responsibilities so readily, who lets his wife spend weeks alone on a remote part of the east coast, without even taking the trouble to come and see if she's all right.'

Olivia stiffened. 'How do you know he hasn't?'

'Because Tom Drake told me you hadn't had any visitors since you got here,' he retorted flatly. 'Believe it or not, but last night he said he was glad I was showing you some attention. He and Eva had been feeling sorry for you——'

Any weakening Olivia might have been feeling towards him vanished. 'How dare you?' she demanded, somehow finding the strength to propel him away from her, and lurching to her feet. 'How dare you?' she said again, clutching back her hair with one hand, and fumbling for the pins that had got caught in her sweater with the other. 'Did you honestly think that telling me you'd been gossiping about me with the landlord would make me feel better? My God! What do you think I am? Are you saying that because I'm disabled you feel some misguided sort of responsibility for me?'

'No!' Conor scowled. 'Hell, Liv...' He got up now, and against her will she noticed that his shirt was half open down his chest. Had she done that? she wondered, half disgustedly, even while her eyes fed greedily on the muscled flesh it exposed. 'I have not been *gossiping* about you with anyone. What Tom Drake said, he said with the best of intentions. God, if you ask me, the Drakes care more about what happens to you than your husband does.'

'But I didn't ask you, did I? And I see now what all this is about,' she added painfully. 'You felt sorry for me, too. Tell me something, does Sharon know you've been spending this evening consoling this poor abandoned female?'

'God!' Conor swore now. 'Haven't you listened to a word I've said? I've told you how I feel about you being here, and Sharon doesn't come into it.' He reached for her arm. 'Goddammit, you know it! This is just you and me!'

'And—Stephen,' put in Olivia recklessly, evading his outstretched hand. She held up her head. 'I forgot to tell you. He arrived this afternoon. He's waiting for me back at the inn.'

Conor's expression ran the whole gamut of emotion from raw frustration to disbelief. 'You're lying.'

'Why would I lie?' she retorted, though there was a tremor in her voice all the same. 'That's why I didn't want you to come into the pub. If you don't believe me, ring Tom Drake. I'm sure he'd be only too pleased to confirm it.'

CHAPTER SEVEN

To OLIVIA'S relief, she didn't see Stephen again until breakfast.

Conor had let her phone for a taxi to bring her back to the hotel, and she had managed to hurry upstairs to her room without anyone noticing her. And she had made sure her light was out before Stephen came up to bed. She was half convinced he had stopped outside her door, but, to her relief, he hadn't attempted to disturb her.

Not that she'd have opened the door anyway, she assured herself tautly. The evening had been quite disastrous enough, without her ex-husband adding his contribution to it. Indeed, she couldn't even remember feeling as shattered as she had done when she arrived back at the inn. And, although she had crawled straight into bed, it was hours before she had got to sleep.

The trouble was that, as soon as she closed her eyes, the events of the evening had replayed themselves endlessly behind her lids, and, no matter how she tried, she couldn't displace the image of Conor's face as she had last seen him.

God, would she ever forget how he had looked when she told him Stephen was waiting for her at the inn? He had tried to deny it, of course, but the fact was she wouldn't have said it, if it couldn't be proved, and he knew it. The bleakness that had descended on his features when he realised she wasn't lying had been positively frightening. And, watching him, what she had desperately wanted to do was retract her words and comfort him. Only the knowledge that it was probably the kindest way to let him down had kept her silent. After all, when she left Paget, she would never see him

102

again. Aside from the fact that she would probably be
a cripple for the rest of her life, she was too old for him.
He needed someone young, and vital. Like Sharon, she
admitted, somewhat ruefully. Someone who could take
what he had to give, without expecting anything in
return. And something told her—in that regard—she had
more to lose than he had...

In consequence, although she would have liked to ask
if she could have breakfast in her room, she squared her
shoulders and went down to the dining-room. If she
wanted to convince the Drakes—and indirectly Conor—
that she and Stephen were still on good terms, she had
to behave as normally as possible. But that didn't stop
her wondering whether she wouldn't be wiser to leave
right away. Stephen knew where she was now, she reminded herself defensively, and, although she didn't
think she was ready to go back to town yet, an alternative
base might be a good idea. She had the uneasy feeling
it would take her a little time to reconcile herself to the
feelings Conor had so effortlessly aroused.

Stephen was already sitting at the window table—
reading her newspaper, she saw indignantly—when she
went downstairs, and it was not without some misgivings that she made her way towards him. Unwillingly,
her mind was already making comparisons between his
puffy eyes and balding head and Conor's masculine
beauty, and she acknowledged it was probably rough
justice, when he remarked, scathingly, 'God, what did
you do with yourself last night? You look grim!'

'Thanks.' Snatching her newspaper out of his hand,
she seated herself opposite, and buried her face in its
pages. She refused to give in to the childish desire to tell
him she had been thinking the same—about him—and
it was left to Stephen to try and make amends.

'Well, you do look pale,' he muttered. 'You don't look
as if you've been to bed at all. Is that leg still giving you
problems?'

'No.'

Olivia resented having to tell him anything, and, as if
losing patience, Stephen reached across the table and
squashed the paper down until he could see her face.
'So, where did you go last night?' he demanded. 'I waited
over an hour for you to show up, and by the time I got
my supper it was cold! I suppose you thought it was
funny, making a fool of me like that in front of the
Drakes!'

Olivia extracted the newspaper from his grasp and
meticulously straightened the pages. 'I didn't give it a
lot of thought,' she admitted honestly. 'And I don't think
I have to give you a résumé of my movements, Stephen.
I went out. Where I went is my affair.'

Stephen scowled. 'I suppose you were with that doctor
and his girlfriend again, weren't you?' he asked, startling
her. 'Oh, yes,' he added, with a mocking smile, 'I've
heard all about *Dr* Brennan. The Drakes didn't know
how you knew him, of course. I think they thought you'd
met him in London, but I put them straight on that ac-
count.' He sneered. 'They were so surprised to hear that
you used to live here.'

Olivia was coldly furious. 'You told them I used to
live in Paget?'

'Yeah.' Stephen lounged back in his chair, enjoying
his triumph. 'Why not? It's not a secret, is it?'

'You had no right...' began Olivia hotly, and then,
realising she was just playing into his hands, she bit off
her words.

But Stephen was not prepared to leave it there. 'Oh,
yes,' he reminisced, 'they were very interested to hear
that you were old Mrs Holland's granddaughter.
Impressed, too, when I told them you were a lady lawyer.
I'd say you were quite a rarity around here. I doubt if
Paget's produced too many lady lawyers.'

Olivia's teeth ground together, and she dug her nails
into her palms to prevent herself from wrapping them
around Stephen's smug neck. In the space of an evening,

he had destroyed all her hard-won anonymity. And as for Conor...

'Yes.' Stephen wouldn't leave it alone. 'You have to admit I've got a good memory. I mean, when the Drakes started talking about *Dr* Brennan, I didn't immediately catch on. But then, I remembered you telling me—soon after we were married, I think it was—about this family who used to live next door to your grandmother. I remembered their name was Brennan, and how the parents were killed, and the son went to live in the United States.' He shrugged modestly. 'Well, as soon as Mrs Drake mentioned that the good doctor had lived in the States before coming back to Paget, I soon put two and two together. Clever, hmm?'

'Masterly,' conceded Olivia contemptuously. 'And while you were telling the Drakes all about my affairs, did you happen to add that you're the low-down ratfink who's been jerking off his boss's wife?'

Stephen's expression was almost comical. He lurched forward in his chair, casting a ludicrously apprehensive look over his shoulder, before snarling angrily, 'Watch your mouth, can't you? For Pete's sake, Harry may have sent someone down here to spy on me, for all I know. It's not as if it was difficult to find out where you were staying. All I did was bribe the caretaker of your apartment building to give me the address you'd left in case of emergencies. Hell, this was an emergency. And Harry could do the same.'

Olivia shook her head. 'So?' she countered, annoyed that Mr Parkinson should have taken Stephen's money. 'Why should I care what happens to you? Maybe Harry would do us both a favour if he shut your mouth for good!'

Stephen blanched. 'You don't mean that, Ollie.'

'Don't I?' Right then, Olivia wasn't too sure. She regarded him without sympathy for a moment, and then added curiously, 'You don't honestly think he would—well, do something criminal, do you?'

'Who knows?' Stephen expelled an unsteady breath. 'If he was mad enough.' He shook his head. 'Oh, I don't know. Maybe he wouldn't go as far as—wiping me out, or anything dramatic like that. But he would make me pay, one way or another.'

'Oh, Stephen——'

'Well, it's true, Ollie. And you know what a low pain threshold I have. I can't bear being hurt; physically hurt, that is. Hell, I faint at the sight of blood! After I'd visited you in hospital that time, when you were all strung up to those IVs and things, I went out and threw up. Literally threw up, and if Darcy's minders get hold of me——'

'Oh, shut up!'

Olivia didn't want to listen to any more. She didn't want to feel responsible. But, much as she despised him, she couldn't stand by and see him beaten up by hooligans. Not that she really believed it would come to that. But, just in case...

Mrs Drake's appearance, to take their orders for breakfast, was as timely as the day before. 'So there you are, Mrs Perry,' she exclaimed. She smiled at Stephen. 'Your husband was quite worried about you last night. Disappearing like that without telling us,' she chided. 'And me making one of my special chicken casseroles for you both.'

'Really?' Olivia folded the newspaper into a neat oblong, and laid it by her plate. 'Well, I'm afraid—Mr Perry—is getting rather absent-minded. I did tell him I had a supper engagement. He must have forgotten to pass it on.'

'Is that right?' Mrs Drake turned to Stephen now, and Olivia was amused to hear him trying to wriggle out of the situation.

'I believe she did say something about going out,' he muttered, red-faced, 'but I thought it was tonight.' He gave Olivia a glowering look. 'Still, no harm done, eh?'

Mrs Drake didn't look as convinced of the veracity of that statement as he seemed to be, but she knew better than to argue with her guests. Instead, she flipped open her notebook and took their orders for breakfast, and, if there was a certain tightness around her mouth as she did so, Olivia was grateful that it averted any discussion of her identity.

When they were alone again, however, Stephen lost no time in voicing his complaints. 'Making me the scapegoat!' he muttered, his mouth a sullen line. 'Why couldn't you have got me an invitation from this bloke Brennan? We could have made up a foursome. I bet that's what the Drakes think.'

'I don't care what the Drakes think,' retorted Olivia shortly, picking up her newspaper again. 'I suggest you think about what time you're leaving. Immediately after breakfast would seem appropriate to me.'

'Oh, would it?' Stephen sounded belligerent at first, but then his shoulders hunched. 'Yes, well—I suppose I will have to go,' he muttered. 'I've got an appointment in Eastbourne at half-past three.'

Olivia looked down at her place mat, not wanting him to see the relief in her eyes. But once Stephen was gone, she intended to make her own arrangements, and this time no one would know her destination.

She was gazing out of the window, wondering if escaping the sight of Stephen ploughing his way through bacon, eggs, sausage and fried potatoes was worth giving up her second cup of coffee for, when someone entered the tiny dining-room. As before, when Stephen himself had interrupted her meal, Olivia expected it to be Mrs Drake. But it wasn't. To her dismay, it was Conor who was crossing the room towards them.

Her sudden intake of breath was clearly audible, and Stephen looked up from his plate. 'Burnt your mouth?' he scoffed, around a mouthful of toast. 'Serves you right. You should eat something, Ollie. Heaven knows, it's not as if you don't need it!'

Olivia looked away from his greasy lips, lifting her head to Conor's dark-skinned face. Oh, God, she thought despairingly, what was he doing, coming here? And why did just the sight of him sing like music in her soul?

Her expression, guarded though it was, alerted Stephen to the fact that they were no longer alone. 'What...?' he began irritably, glancing round. And then, as the other man came to stand beside their table, he put down his knife and fork, and wiped his face with a nervous hand. 'What do you want?'

It came to Olivia in a flash that Stephen was actually alarmed. He was sweating profusely, and his fair skin was red and blotchy. The contrast between his hot agitation and Conor's calm self-possession could not have been more pronounced, and she was sorely tempted to let him stew. It was obvious he thought Conor must work for Harry Darcy, and if she had had any doubts that he had been exaggerating his fears they were quickly extinguished.

'I said, what do you——?' Stephen was beginning again, shoving back his chair and getting unsteadily to his feet, but, before Olivia could speak, Conor took the initiative.

'I'm Conor Brennan,' he said coolly, offering his hand. 'A friend of—your wife's. And you must be Stephen.'

It was only then that Olivia remembered what she had told Conor. Here she was, enjoying Stephen's discomfort, and any minute he was going to tell the other man that they were divorced. She sighed. Oh, why had Conor come here? A phone call would have been enough to ensure that she wasn't lying about Stephen's visit.

Stephen had stopped blustering, and he shook the other man's hand almost automatically. But his eyes were definitely suspicious. 'You're—*Dr* Brennan,' he exclaimed, his eyes flicking back and forth between Conor and Olivia. 'You're the family friend she had dinner with last night?'

'That's right.' Conor thrust both hands into the pockets of his black leather jacket. He was all in black again today—black jacket, black trousers, his black shirt buttoned to the collar. But no tie, she noticed almost illogically. Yet, she thought, he looked so much better than Stephen in his business suit.

'I understand you've just arrived from London,' Conor continued politely. 'Are you staying long?'

Stephen frowned, and Olivia guessed he was wondering how much she had told Conor about their situation. Not nearly enough, she thought uneasily, not really wanting Stephen to know she had lied about their relationship.

'Stephen's leaving this morning,' she put in hurriedly, glad she was sitting down when she said it. When Conor turned those clear green eyes on her, her legs felt distinctly wobbly. And it had nothing to do with the accident.

'Really?' Conor's expression was unreadable. He turned back to Stephen. 'Just a flying visit, then?'

Stephen hesitated a moment, and then resumed his seat. 'In a manner of speaking,' he said, looking thoughtfully at his ex-wife. He put a forkful of fried potato into his mouth, and his eyes narrowed speculatively. 'I had to come and see how my—wife—was faring, didn't I? It was good of you to look after her, Brennan. Ollie's had a hard time of it lately, and there aren't many young chaps, like yourself, willing to spend an evening cheering up an old friend of their mother's.'

Olivia's face flamed. She couldn't help it. And resentment that Stephen should talk about her as if she were some decrepit old crock brought her to the point of revealing exactly how unaltruistic Conor's motives had been.

But, once again, it was Conor who saved her from herself. 'It's my pleasure,' he said smoothly, and Olivia wondered if she was only imagining the thread of steel in his voice. 'And I don't regard Liv as just a friend of my mother's. We grew up together.'

'Oh, come on.' Stephen had recovered himself now, and his smile was openly disparaging. 'That's carrying chivalry a bit far, don't you think? Ollie's years older than you are.'

Conor's features hardened. 'Well, no one could accuse you of an excess of chivalry, could they?' he retorted, and, although the words were undeniably offensive, they were delivered in such an even tone that Stephen was clearly unsure how to take them.

His uncertainty was transparent in the suspicious face he turned up to the other man, but apparently discretion got the better part of valour. 'Yeah, well—there's no point in avoiding the facts,' he muttered, evidently deciding that in any physical contest between them he'd come out the loser. 'Say it how it is—that's been my motto in life. And I haven't done too badly, all things considered.'

Conor's contempt was almost tangible. 'You think not?' he remarked, with a wintry smile. 'Then I'm sure you'll appreciate my reasons for saying that, as far as I can see, you don't give a shit about anyone but yourself!'

Stephen's jaw sagged, and Olivia was treated to a sickening view of half-masticated food. But that was a minor misfortune compared to the reaction Conor's words had evoked. There was no way Stephen could ignore the insult this time, and her heart sank convulsively as he struggled to find his feet.

'Just who do you think you're talking to?' he demanded incredulously. 'Look——' he wiped his face on his napkin and threw it down on the table '—I don't know what lies Ollie's been telling you, son, but take it from me—you don't know what the hell you're talking about.'

'Don't I?'

Conor hadn't even taken his hands out of his pockets. He just stood there, eye to eye with the other man, a vaguely insolent smirk on his lean features, and Olivia wanted to die. What did he think he was doing? she fretted anxiously. Her ex-husband might be a coward, if the odds were stacked against him, but he might not be able to resist taking a pot-shot at such an unguarded target.

'Aw, hell!' Stephen snorted. 'What are you trying to do? Pick a fight with me?' He spread his hands. 'Why? What's Ollie to you?'

'That's enough!' Almost overbalancing her chair, Olivia rose and pushed herself between them. 'It's barely nine o'clock in the morning, do you realise that? You haven't even got the excuse that you've been drinking. How do you think Mrs Drake will react, if she comes back and finds you two brawling?'

'Well, it's not my fault,' retorted Stephen, and, although she knew Conor had only been defending what he thought were her rights, Olivia had to agree with him. 'You'd better get your—*boy*friend to apologise,' he added balefully, and she was relieved to hear that he was willing to back down.

'In a pig's eye,' remarked Conor distinctly, and Olivia's stomach hollowed. 'I meant every word I said.'

Stephen gazed at him disbelievingly, and Olivia had to admit she shared a little of his incredulity. What was Conor trying to do? she wondered anxiously. Force the other man to attack him?

There was a moment when she thought he had driven Stephen too far, but evidently her ex-husband was not prepared to risk physical violence. 'I think you'd better go,' he said, and she guessed he was hoping Conor would take his victory with good grace. 'I'm going to do us both a favour and forget this ever happened. And if you want to continue working in this country, I suggest you do the same.'

Conor's mouth twisted, and Olivia just knew he wasn't going to let it go at that. 'Oh?' he said scornfully. 'Why?'

Stephen lifted his chin. 'I should have thought that was obvious. The British Medical Association don't take kindly to their practitioners behaving like hooligans, threatening decent, law-abiding citizens.'

Conor lifted his shoulders, indicating his hands were still in his pockets. 'Am I threatening you?' He shrugged. 'I can't help it if you don't like your own medicine—if you'll forgive the pun.'

Stephen looked at Olivia now, and she could see the anger and resentment he was trying so hard to disguise. 'What the hell have you been telling him?' he demanded, and she guessed that if they had been alone his words would have been much stronger. 'For God's sake, I wasn't responsible for the accident. If you'd spent less time in the office, and more with me, you wouldn't be in this mess!'

Olivia put an involuntary hand to her throat. She didn't know whether she was dismayed or relieved that he had so obviously misunderstood Conor's motives. But before she could make any response, Conor's hands came to grip her upper arms, and, although at first she was afraid he was going to remove the barrier she represented, he spun her round to face him.

'Get your coat, Liv,' he said, his eyes glittering with some unidentifiable emotion. 'Go on. I'll wait outside in the car.'

'My—coat?' Olivia was confused.

'Yes. I'm taking you out,' he said, his gaze flicking briefly to Stephen, as if daring him to challenge his statement. 'Don't worry. I won't touch him while you're gone.'

'The hell you won't!' snarled Stephen belligerently, but Olivia knew he wouldn't do anything now. He'd had his chance, and ducked it. Nevertheless, he was determined to have the last word. 'Well, well, well,' he sneered. 'So that's the way it is.'

'Shut your mouth, Perry.' Conor kept his tone polite, but there was no mistaking the underlying note of menace. He looked at Olivia. 'Well, what are you waiting for?'

Olivia shook her head. 'I don't think——'

'So, don't,' cut in Conor flatly, turning her round and pointing her towards the door. 'Or do you want me to get it for you?'

'No...' Olivia glanced between the two men. 'No, I'll do it,' she said, somewhat unwillingly. But the situation wasn't of her choosing. What price her eager plans to leave now?

As if sensing her unwillingness to leave them alone, Conor followed her out into the hallway. 'Don't be long,' he said, striding towards the outer door. And, in spite of her misgivings, Olivia found herself going obediently up the stairs.

She was renewing her lipstick with a slightly unsteady hand when the bedroom door opened and Stephen stepped into the room. He stood there, watching her outlining her lips with the red gloss, his expression mirroring his resentment. And, although she knew she ought to object, she couldn't think of a thing to say.

'So, how long has this been going on?' he demanded at last, and the sheer effrontery of his question brought her quickly to her feet.

'There's nothing going on,' she said, putting the cap back on the lipstick and reaching for her hairbrush. 'Get out of my room, Stephen. We have nothing to say to one another.'

'I disagree.' Stephen made an aggressive move, but then, as if realising that wasn't the way to get her attention, he tucked his hands into his trouser pockets and rocked back on his heels. 'In a hurry, aren't you?' he sneered. 'I would be, too, if I had someone young enough to be my daughter panting after me!'

Olivia ground her teeth. 'You're disgusting!'

'Am I?' Stephen's lips curled. 'I wondered why you came to this God-forsaken place. Now I know, don't I?'

'Will you get out of here?' Olivia could hear her voice rising and struggled to hold it down. 'Don't judge everyone by your own standards. Conor and I are friends. Friends, that's all. A man and woman can be friends, although I doubt that's something you know anything about.'

Yet, even as she said the words, Olivia knew herself for the hypocrite she was. How could she dismiss what had happened last night as a 'friendly' encounter? If she hadn't come to her senses when she did, heaven alone knew what might have happened.

Which was why her tone was less than confrontational when she added, 'Just for the record, I didn't know Conor had come back to live in Paget when I came here. I thought the Brennans' house had been sold years ago.' She held up her head. 'But it hadn't.'

'And you just happened to run into him?' suggested Stephen sceptically, and she nodded.

'Yes.'

Stephen was silent for so long that she was sure he was trying to read her mind. But it wasn't really a lie, she told herself defensively. Though not quite the truth either, she conceded with a sigh.

'All right.' To her relief, Stephen seemed to accept her explanation. 'So what's going on?'

'Going on?'

'Yes, going on.' Stephen dipped his head in the direction of the front of the inn. 'You can't seriously pretend you don't know what he's after.'

'Stephen, please!'

'Well, it's the truth.' Stephen scowled. 'And you're a fool if you think he's serious about you. Hell, I don't want to hurt you, Ollie, but take a look at yourself. You're a woman, approaching middle age, to whom fate hasn't exactly been kind. Oh, you've got nice hair, and nice eyes, and you used to have nice legs before——'

'Yes, thank you.'

Olivia cut him off before he could go any further. But there was a tremor in her voice as she did so, and she despised herself for allowing anything he said to upset her. Whatever else, his comments were not unbiased, and she hated the thought that he might detect her weakness.

'Well——' Stephen shrugged now '—all I'm saying is that you're not someone he'd get seriously involved with. I mean—he's young, and even I can see that he'd attract the birds. But you're not a bird, Ollie. You're someone he's known since he was a kid, and he feels sorry for you. Maybe he does think you've had a rough time. He may have some justification for thinking I walked out on you just when you needed me most. But, hell—I didn't know how things were going to turn out. I never wanted this divorce, remember? I hope you told him that.'

Olivia moistened her lips. 'I think you'd better go.'

'OK.' To her relief, he didn't argue. 'But think about what I've said, Ollie. You're an intelligent woman. You know it makes sense.'

'Stephen——'

'All right, all right.' He sauntered towards the door. 'So—I'll be seeing you, right?'

Not if I see you first, muttered Olivia under her breath, and then felt the hot sting of tears behind her eyes. Damn him, she thought painfully, crossing the room and slamming the door behind him. Why did he have to be right?

CHAPTER EIGHT

ONLY the thought that Conor might get tired of waiting and come looking for her forced Olivia to collect her coat and go downstairs. But she had no intention of going out with him, she told herself severely, as she checked the knot of hair at her nape. She would just tell him she had a headache—*more lies!*—and get rid of him.

The Audi was parked at the front entrance, with Conor at the wheel. When she emerged from the inn, he thrust open the door from inside, as he had done the night before. 'Get in.'

'No.' Olivia hung back. 'I—er—I've just come to tell you I've got a headache. I'm going to take a couple of capsules and rest for a while on the bed.'

Conor's mouth compressed. 'I said, get in,' he repeated, and she could tell he didn't believe a word. 'Or do you want me to get out and force you into the car?'

Olivia stood back. 'You wouldn't dare.'

Conor said nothing more. He just thrust open his door, and, rather than scuttle back inside like a frightened rabbit, Olivia said, 'Oh, all right,' and scrambled into the seat beside him.

But, if she'd thought that Conor might give her a few minutes to think of another excuse, she was wrong. As soon as she was inside the car and the door closed, he took off at speed, the rear of the car fish-tailing briefly, before maintaining its grip on the icy road.

'Are you crazy?' she exclaimed, groping for her seatbelt, and he immediately eased his foot off the accelerator.

'Sorry,' he muttered ruefully. 'I guess that was a bit thoughtless. Did I drive too fast last night? Was that why you wouldn't let me bring you home?'

'You know why I got a taxi back last night,' retorted Olivia shortly, and Conor lifted one shoulder.

'Oh, sure. I'd been drinking,' he conceded calmly. 'And you didn't want me to lose my licence, right?'

Olivia only glared at him, not prepared to go any further with that particular argument. 'Why did you come to the inn this morning?' she demanded. 'You knew Stephen would be there. What did you hope to prove?'

'That you're not happy with him?' suggested Conor, less flippantly. 'I know. You're mad at me. But, dammit, I didn't start it.'

Olivia's expression didn't change. 'You are joking.'

'No.' Conor's hands tightened on the wheel. 'Hell, Liv, how could you marry that moron?'

'Stephen's not a moron.' Hardly aware of why she was doing so, Olivia found herself defending him. 'He's just—unthinking sometimes.'

'He's a creep!' muttered Conor, without compassion. 'When he said what he did about the accident, I wanted to stuff my fist down his throat.'

'Yes.' Olivia swallowed. 'Yes, I think he—we—all—knew that.' She licked her dry lips. 'But—he's right, you know. It's not your problem.'

Conor glanced her way. 'And if I choose to make it my problem?'

'You can't.'

'Why can't I?'

Olivia shook her head. 'You had no right to speak to Stephen as you did. My God, you were deliberately trying to provoke him. And he's right, you know. The BMA would view your behaviour very unsympathetically.'

'To hell with the BMA,' responded Conor succinctly. 'And as far as your husband is concerned, I consider I acted with remarkable restraint, in the circumstances.'

'Well, I don't.' Olivia frowned, and then added with some reluctance, "What circumstances?"'

Conor glanced her way. 'Last night,' he said evenly.

Olivia turned her head towards the window. 'Where are you taking me?' she asked, refusing to consider what he might mean by that. Besides, while she had been caught up in their conversation, Conor had driven out of the village. They were on the coast road now, heading towards Witterthorpe, with Pagwell Priory looming out of the mist.

'Liv...' Conor removed one hand from the wheel, and covered both of hers, which were curled tightly in her lap. 'Liv,' he repeated softly, 'don't shut me out. I need to know how you feel about that—about Stephen.'

His fingers brushed her thigh, her muscles taut beneath the velvet Lycra of her leggings. She had an insane urge to part her legs and crush his hand between them. God, she wanted him to touch her there, just as he had done the night before. What on earth was the matter with her? She'd never felt like this before.

'Talk to me, dammit. I have a right to know.'

Conor's words broke the feeling of self-absorption that had been gripping her. Abruptly, she pushed his hand away, and pressed her legs together. 'You have no rights where I'm concerned,' she retorted. 'None at all. Now—are you going to tell me where we're going, or is this another silly game?'

Conor's jaw compressed. 'I have to call at the clinic,' he said, and Olivia's lips parted.

'The rehabilitation clinic in Witterthorpe?' she exclaimed, and Conor inclined his head.

'Unless you know of another,' he remarked sardonically, looking at her mouth. 'Don't worry. I won't keep you long. I just have to check on the patient who delayed me last night.'

Olivia felt his gaze as if it were something tangible, and for a moment she couldn't say anything. But then, in spite of her unwillingness to get involved in his life, curiosity got the better of her. 'The emergency?' she ventured, as he looked back at the road. 'What happened? Can you tell me about it?'

'I could.' Conor spoke carelessly. 'But you probably wouldn't be interested.'

Olivia sighed. 'Why not?'

Conor gave her an old-fashioned look. 'Come on. You've spent the last fifteen minutes showing me that you're not interested in anything about me, that you care about your husband, and that I'm just wasting my time trying to get through to you. Well, OK. If that's the way you want it, there's not a lot I can do about it. I may not like it, and, whatever you say, last night you did want me just as much as I wanted you. But—you are married, and I guess I have to respect that.'

Olivia's chin scrubbed the collar of her blouse. She had worn a blouse this morning, a cream blouse with a round collar, together with a long honey-brown cardigan that skimmed the tops of her thighs. Over this, she was presently wearing her cashmere coat—unbuttoned and gaping open, it was true, but very warm just the same.

Which was why she suddenly felt hot all over, she decided unsteadily, smoothing her damp palms over her knees. It wasn't what Conor had said, or the empty feeling she had experienced when she had realised he was backing off. It was just the warmth of her clothes, and the heat of the car, and the undeniable nearness of his body.

'Right?' he asked now, glancing her way again, and she nodded rather vigorously.

'Oh—right,' she echoed sturdily, transferring her attention to the window again. This was what she wanted, wasn't it? And why shouldn't she use Stephen to achieve her ends? He hadn't hesitated in doing the same.

The clinic was situated on the outskirts of the small market town. It had originally been the gynaecological unit of the Witterthorpe General Hospital, Conor told her, but when a new obstetric wing had been built the older building had been utilised as a rehabilitation centre.

'The facilities aren't exactly custom-made,' he added, parking the Audi in one of the staff bays. 'You'd better come in. You can wait in my office.'

Olivia understood what he meant as soon as she entered the building. In spite of the freshly painted walls and bright tubular furniture in the waiting-room, the long, draughty corridors and lofty ceilings were distinctly Victorian in appearance. She guessed it must cost a fortune just to heat this place, and at this hour of the morning the radiators were not winning the battle. As well as feeling chilly, there was also a distinctive smell of antiseptic in the air, and the memories it evoked were not welcome.

Conor regarded her wrinkled nose with thin-lipped resignation, however. 'Perhaps you'd better wait in the car,' he said, and she knew he hadn't connected her expression with the prolonged spell she had spent in a hospital just like this.

'It's all right,' she said, ignoring her queasy stomach, and tipping up the collar of her coat. 'Which way is your office? I hope you've got a heater.'

The receptionist greeted Conor warmly, but her eyes lingered longer on his companion. Olivia realised she was probably being assessed as a prospective patient. She doubted the manicured blonde behind the desk would mistake her for anything else.

The corridor had been carpeted, no doubt to help dispel the atmosphere of a hospital ward, and Conor walked more quickly than Olivia. It meant that he had to stop and wait for her to catch up, and she automatically quickened her step, to escape his probing eyes.

'Shit,' he said, as she reached him. 'You must think I'm a thoughtless bastard! That's why you looked so sick when we came in. I should have realised a place like this would bring back memories you'd rather forget.'

Olivia tucked her hands deeply into her pockets, as two women and a man emerged from a room further along on the right. 'I can live with it,' she said lightly, and hoped that Conor wouldn't feel the need to introduce her to his colleagues.

'But can I?' he responded obliquely, reaching naturally for her arm, and drawing her aside. 'Anyway, it's not much further now. And, yes, I do have an electric heater.'

To her relief, the three members of staff—whose only means of identification were the plastic-covered name tags, showing their picture, that they wore on their lapels—didn't have time for a prolonged conversation. The talk was all of some youth, who had apparently nearly killed himself the day before. It seemed he had taken an overdose of a substance known as 'crack', and Olivia, who knew exactly how dangerous a drug it was, wondered what it was doing here, in an establishment dedicated to its destruction.

Nevertheless, in spite of the seriousness of the topic, Olivia found herself watching Conor almost compulsively. Here, among his peers, she was seeing him in a different light, and she knew an undeserved sense of pride in his achievement. He spoke to the others so confidently, his manner relaxed, his knowledge undeniable. The two women were obviously older than he was, and yet they seemed to defer to his opinion. It made Olivia realise that age was not necessarily synonymous with ability—or with intelligence either, she reflected ruefully, thinking of Stephen.

She did wonder who they thought she was, and she guessed they were curious, too, in spite of everything. Particularly the women. Were these two of the 'manhunters' Sharon had spoken about? Olivia speculated drily. Somehow she doubted it. She suspected that most women enjoyed the company of an attractive man. And just because these women were doctors they weren't immune from the condition. Sharon had just been warning her off—not in the most subtle way imaginable.

In any event, Conor excused himself before any lapse in the conversation could leave room for unwanted questions. With polite smiles all round, the two groups separated, and Olivia was relieved when they reached a door bearing the legend, *C. Brennan, M.D.*

She touched the nameplate as she passed, running her fingers over the letters almost wonderingly. Sally and Keith would have been so pleased, she thought, feeling almost tearful for a moment. But then she met Conor's inscrutable gaze, and she hastily disguised her emotions.

His office—or was it a consulting room? she wondered—was infinitely more inviting than the corridor outside. The walls here were hung with posters, and the carpet underfoot was plum-coloured and attractive. There was a desk, but there was also a couch and two armchairs, forming a kind of conversation piece in one corner. And there was a rubber plant, and a winter-flowering poinsettia, all adding to the impression of a secular apartment.

'This is nice,' she said, looking round, as he riffled through the papers—messages?—on his desk. She gestured towards the plants. 'Did—er—did Sharon get these for you?'

Conor was standing behind his desk, but now he looked up with a trace of impatience. 'What? Oh, no. The rubber plant was already here when I arrived, and Aunt Elizabeth sent me the poinsettia at Christmas. To remind me of home,' he added drily. 'She still regards Florida as my home.'

Olivia couldn't help herself. 'Do *you*?'

'No.' Conor's eyes were hard. 'I've told you,' he said tersely. 'Paget is my home.' He straightened the papers he had been scanning and came round the desk again. 'Now I've got to go. You'll be all right here. I'll have one of the nurses bring you some coffee.'

Olivia hesitated. 'I—couldn't help overhearing what you were saying just now.' She nodded her head towards the corridor outside. 'Is that right? One of your patients took an overdose?'

Conor's mouth twisted. 'I guess so.'

'But——' Olivia lifted her shoulders '—how could that happen?'

Conor shrugged. 'Someone supplied the stuff,' he said carelessly. 'It happens.'

'Someone on the staff?'

'Could be.'

Olivia shook her head. 'How could they?'

'Try money,' remarked Conor, taking his own identity tag out of his pocket, and making for the door. 'I won't be long.'

Olivia found herself going after him. 'There's no— danger—is there?' she ventured, suddenly reluctant to let him go, and Conor's eyes softened.

'Not to me,' he assured her gently, putting out his hand and looping an errant strand of hair behind her ear. 'You'll wait for me, hmm?'

Olivia pulled a wry face. 'Do I have a choice?'

'Well, you could call a cab,' he remarked flatly, and she wondered why that hadn't occurred to her. 'But you won't,' he appended, holding her gaze. 'You're going to give us both the pleasure of letting me drive you home.'

Of course, after he had left her, she thought of all the things she should have said to him. Not least, a reminder that his behaviour was hardly fair to Stephen. If they had still been married, how would she have reacted then? It was disturbing to discover she was ambivalent about her answer.

But it was difficult to feel any obligation towards Stephen, real or imaginary, she defended herself. His actions had hardly been honourable, and her only real loyalty was to Sally's memory. But it was becoming equally difficult to keep that in mind, even if she suspected Conor's attraction to her was rooted in the past.

She had turned on the electric fan to supplement the heat coming from the radiator, and was sitting at Conor's desk flicking idly through a copy of the *Lancet* when the door opened. She thought perhaps there had been a knock first, albeit a perfunctory one, but, before she could answer, the door had opened and a woman came into the room.

She was a middle-aged woman—in her late forties, Olivia estimated—with permed blonde hair, liberally streaked with grey. She was wearing a white overall, unbuttoned at the neck to reveal the lacy jabot of a hot pink blouse, and rather unsuitable high heels. She was also carrying a polystyrene cup of coffee, which she set down on the desk rather heavily, causing some to splash over Conor's papers.

Olivia snatched a tissue from her pocket to mop up the steaming liquid, but, even as she did so, she was struck by the woman's familiarity. She bore a striking resemblance to someone she had seen recently, and only as comprehension dawned did the possible reasons for the woman's vaguely hostile stare become apparent. Mrs Drake had told her that Sharon's mother worked at the clinic. And this woman was simply an older version of her daughter.

'Thank you,' she said now, feeling awkward for no reason, and wondered whether she ought to mention the resemblance. But, before she could make up her mind, Mrs Holmes forestalled her.

'Milk, but no sugar,' she said, indicating the slightly murky-looking liquid in the cup. 'We don't keep those sachets of sugar on the premises, for obvious reasons. But I believe Conor keeps a supply of sugar in his drawer, if you want some.'

'No.' Olivia dropped the damp tissue into the waste bin and held up her hand. 'No, this is fine,' she assured her. 'I don't take sugar.'

'No, I thought not,' observed the other woman, with all her daughter's discretion. 'Still, not many people do nowadays. It's like smoking. It's going out of fashion.'

Olivia was tempted to say that fashion had little to do with the decline in smoking, but she had no wish to get into an argument with the woman. Besides, everyone was entitled to their own opinion.

'You're Mrs Perry, aren't you?' the woman continued now. 'Sharon's told me all about you. Oh—I'm Sharon's mother, by the way. Mrs Holmes.'

Olivia's lips twitched a little at the form the introduction had taken. But then, guessing that the woman was probably waiting for her to taste the coffee, she wrapped her cold hands around the warm cup. The insulation kept the hot coffee from burning her fingers as she brought it to her lips, and she took a tentative mouthful, before adding, 'Mmm, that's good.'

Mrs Holmes folded her arms across her midriff. 'Sharon says you're here on holiday,' she remarked, and Olivia realised her hopes of being left alone had been premature. So far as Sharon's mother was concerned, her daughter's relationship with Conor gave her the right to interrogate his friends. 'Funny place to come for a holiday, isn't it? I mean—at this time of the year.'

Olivia took another sip of the coffee. It wasn't as good as she had implied, and it tasted of powdered milk. But it did give her a few moments to think of a response, and Mrs Holmes seemed to wilt in the vacuum.

'Well,' Olivia said at last, 'I used to live in Paget, you see. And—it seemed as good a place as any to relax.'

Mrs Holmes sniffed. 'I can think of better places,' she muttered. Then, changing tack, 'I suppose it's nice for you, seeing Conor again. I imagine you've seen quite a change in him. He was just a boy when you saw him last, wasn't he?'

Olivia pressed her lips together. 'Something like that,' she conceded after a moment, beginning to resent this questioning. For heaven's sake, had Mrs Holmes appointed herself Conor's keeper?

'Of course, we're all very fond of him here,' the woman went on, her voice starting to grate on Olivia's nerves. 'Professor Marshall—he's the chief administrator—he speaks very highly of Conor's abilities. He's hoping he'll stay here. He's got a real—a real—oh, you know! With the patients?'

'Rapport?'

'Yes, that's it.' The woman nodded. 'A real rapport with them. They talk to him, when they won't talk to anyone else. I think it's because he's so close to them in age. It makes a difference, you know. Don't you agree?'

'Oh—sure.'

Olivia could hear the edge in her voice, but she couldn't help it. And, anyway, Mrs Holmes wasn't listening to her.

'Yes,' she went on, cupping her elbow with one hand and resting her chin on the heel of the other, 'you forget sometimes how young he is. Oh, but he's had Sharon's dad and me in stitches a dozen times, talking about his student days.' She laughed reminiscently, and Olivia wanted to slap her. 'Those interns! It's a wonder any of their patients survived!'

Olivia finished her coffee with a convulsive swallow, and allowed the empty cup to join the tissue in the waste bin. It seemed a shame to soil the bin, which, until she had used it, had been pristine. Perhaps she should ask Mrs Holmes to empty it, she thought maliciously, and then chided herself for permitting such a thought.

But the picture of family domesticity the woman was painting rankled. She could tell herself it was a deliberate attempt to show Conor's relationship with Sharon in another light, but she still felt annoyed. Why bother? she wondered irritably. Did they really think she was some kind of threat?

'Anyway,' Mrs Holmes continued smugly, 'I suppose I'd better be getting on. It's been nice talking to you, Mrs Perry, but I really shouldn't waste any more time.'

Another dig? Olivia's smile was thin. Who asked you to? she wanted to say childishly. She'd just as soon have missed out on this enlightening experience.

'Did Conor bring you here?' the woman probed, as she did a kind of sideways *chassé* to the door, and Olivia wondered, for the first time, what Conor had told her. How had he conveyed the news that he had brought a visitor to the clinic? And what excuse had he given for bringing her here in the first place?

But, 'Yes,' she responded now, not prepared to prevaricate. 'He—um—had a patient he wanted to see.'

'Oh—Stuart Henley, yes.' To Olivia's dismay, Mrs Holmes lingered. 'The silly fool nearly killed himself inhaling a mixture of crack and baking powder. Do you know, his heart stopped beating! If it hadn't been for Conor, he'd be dead or brain-damaged or something.'

Olivia found her breath catching the back of her throat. 'But—he's all right now?' she murmured tensely, sure she shouldn't be asking Mrs Holmes the question, but unable to prevent herself just the same.

'He's still alive,' agreed Sharon's mother, with the air of someone who'd played a crucial part in his survival. 'These kids! They don't have any sense. Thank heavens my Sharon's never got involved in anything like that.'

'Mmm.'

Olivia couldn't argue with her there, and, to her relief, Mrs Holmes reached for the handle of the door.

'I'd better go,' she said once again. 'I've got work to do.'

Olivia managed a thin smile. 'I'm sure.'

'You—er—you'll have to get Conor to bring you over to tea one day,' she continued, as she swung the door open. 'I'll tell our Sharon to fix it up, shall I? It'll give you a bit of company, won't it? And I'm sure Sharon's dad would like to meet an old friend of Conor's parents.'

CHAPTER NINE

OLIVIA was standing staring out of the window when Conor came back. She had been sitting down; she supposed she should still be sitting down. But Sharon's mother had made her so mad that she couldn't wait to get out of there.

She knew she was a fool, letting the other woman get under her skin, but that final dig about Conor's parents had been the last straw. Good God, she was not that old! If Sally and Keith had still been alive they'd have been forty-six and forty-eight respectively. She was thirty-four! Eight years older than Conor, it was true, but not their contemporary.

She was attempting to admire the clumps of daffodils growing wild beside the footpath, when Conor came into the room. Unlike Mrs Holmes, he hadn't knocked, but the face she turned towards him was still vaguely apprehensive.

And he knew instantly that something had happened. 'What is it?' he asked, with some resignation, closing the door with his shoulders, and slipping the pen he had been holding back into his pocket. 'Didn't anyone bring you any coffee?'

Olivia's mouth thinned. 'Oh, yes,' she said, slipping her hands back into their pockets and propping her hips against the sill. 'A Mrs Holmes attended to it.' Her wintry smile was ironic. 'I think she wanted to check me out.'

'Oh, God!' Conor swore. 'How did she find out you were here?'

'Who knows?' Olivia was dismissive. 'Are you ready to leave? Because if not——'

'I'm ready. I'm ready.' Conor pushed himself away from the door, and glanced half impatiently about the room. 'I gather she came back to collect the tray.'

'What tray?' Olivia propelled herself up from the window-sill. 'You don't need a tray for a disposable cup.'

Conor exhaled almost wearily. 'Connie must have been desperate,' he remarked, walking across to his desk. He pulled a folder out of a drawer, and, sorting through the papers on the desk, he stuffed some of them into it. His hands encountered the damp pages Olivia had tried so hard to sponge dry, and he gave her a wry look. 'What did she do? Throw it at you?'

Olivia had to smile. 'Something like that,' she admitted ruefully, moving over to join him. 'Is anything spoiled?'

'No.' Conor was laconic. 'But, believe it or not, I did ask one of the nurses to make the coffee. Real coffee, not that machine crap.'

'It doesn't matter.' Olivia shrugged. 'So—how is he?'

Conor widened his eyes. 'How do you know it's a he?'

Olivia grinned. 'I even know his name. Your Mrs Holmes is very chatty.'

'She's not *my* Mrs Holmes.'

'Well, *your* Sharon's mother, then,' declared Olivia equably. 'Once she'd assured herself I wasn't a threat to your relationship, she became quite friendly.'

Conor's mouth turned down. 'Did she?'

'Hmm.' Olivia found it was quite enjoyable to turn the tables on him for a change. 'She's even invited me over to their house for tea. She says she'll get Sharon to fix it up with you.'

Conor's mouth compressed. 'I don't think so.'

'Oh?' Olivia feigned disappointment. 'Why not?'

'Because I don't expect to be seeing Sharon again,' he told her shortly, and she was still absorbing this statement when his arm looped about her shoulders, dragging her towards him. 'I'd stop inviting trouble, if I were you,' he added, his hot breath moistening her ear. 'That is, unless you're prepared to take the consequences.'

Olivia pulled away from him at once, and he let her. But she had no illusions that, had he not wished to let her go, she wouldn't have succeeded. As it was, she was red-faced and eager to change the subject, and her, 'You—you didn't say how the boy is?' was a desperate attempt to rescue her composure.

Conor picked up the folder from the desk. 'He's off the respirator and he's stable,' he replied, much to her relief. But it was mostly relief that he hadn't pursued his earlier statement, rather than concern for someone she didn't know.

'And—did you find out where he got the stuff?' she persisted, and Conor gave her a look that said he knew exactly what she was doing.

But, humouring her, he explained that his patients had visitors, that this wasn't a prison, and that, although security measures were taken, sometimes the system broke down.

'We may never find out where he got it from,' he declared, and when he moved she hastened awkwardly towards the door. 'So let's go and get ourselves some decent coffee.' His smile was faintly malicious. 'And perhaps I should hear some more about this— friendship—you've struck up with Sharon's mother.'

Olivia had forgotten how cold it actually was until she got outside, and then she was quite glad to tuck herself into Conor's car. If his obvious amusement at her discomfort irritated her at all, she was not prepared to pursue it, and she had settled comfortably in her seat when he got in beside her.

'Am I forgiven?'

His first words startled her, and she turned her head to look at him in some surprise. 'For what?'

Conor flicked the key in the ignition, and put the Audi into gear. 'Well, not for teasing you about Connie,' he remarked, releasing the hand-brake, and reversing out of the parking bay. 'I meant——' he glanced her way '—for upsetting your husband.'

'Oh.' Olivia's fingers linked convulsively. 'I—perhaps you should ask Stephen.'

'I don't want to ask Stephen,' retorted Conor tersely, accelerating to the gates of the clinic, and turning out on to the main road. 'Perhaps I should have phrased that differently.' He paused. 'I'm not sorry for what I said. I meant every word. But—dammit—it's obvious your marriage is having problems as it is, and I guess I and my big mouth will only have added to them.'

Olivia glanced his way. 'Why—why do you think my marriage is having problems?' she asked sharply.

'Call it intuition.' Conor was sardonic. 'Hell, Liv, I have had some experience in these situations.'

'I bet you have.'

Her tone was bitter, and he uttered an angry expletive. 'Not from a personal standpoint,' he retorted harshly. 'But I have counselled enough adults to know what goes on.'

Olivia shrugged. 'So what am I supposed to forgive you for?'

'I don't know.' Conor was resentful. 'You twist my words so much, I don't know what the hell I mean.'

'Then perhaps we shouldn't talk about it,' she said, turning her attention back to the scene outside the car's windows. 'Oh, look—it's starting to snow.'

'We have to talk about it,' stated Conor grimly, and she was glad the icy roads meant he had to keep his hands on the wheel. 'If you and Stephen aren't having problems, why did you agree to have supper with me last night?'

Olivia sighed. 'All right. I suppose I should have told you sooner——'

'That's not what I meant, and you know it.' Conor was savage. 'Dammit, Liv, stop treating me like an idiot. If you're not happy, you've got to do something about it.'

'Why?'

She deliberately kept her face turned away from him, but she heard his harsh intake of breath. 'Because of us,' he responded, and she could feel his eyes boring into her back. 'Because if there's any chance of you divorcing him, I want to know about it.'

Olivia expelled her breath as quickly as he had sucked his in. 'Really?' she exclaimed, striving for a mocking tone. Steeling herself, she turned and looked at him. 'Why? Are you going to offer to counsel us?'

'Liv!' Conor's expression was ominous. 'Don't do this. You know what I'm talking about. I don't have to explain. God—you have to know how I feel about you. I've been trying to tell you since I was sixteen years old——'

'No!' Olivia tried to stop him. 'Conor, stop this! I don't find it at all amusing!'

'And you think I do?' he countered, swinging the car too violently round a corner, and having to hang on to the wheel until it righted itself again. 'Hell, Liv, I can't remember a time when you haven't played a part in my life. OK, I had some growing up to do, I accept that. And I also accept that when I came to London to see you, I played it all wrong. But God—I didn't have my head straight in those days. I thought I knew it all, but I didn't.'

'Oh, Conor——'

'No, hear me out, Liv. I was a fool, I know that. I got involved in things you don't want to know about. But that's all over now. I'm all grown-up. I'm a man, Liv, and I know what I want.'

'Not—me——'

'Why not you?' His eyes darkened as they rested briefly on her mouth. 'I don't believe you don't feel something for me.'

'Well, I do, of course——'

'You do?'

'—but not—not in that way,' she protested, anxious to convince herself as well as him. 'Conor, whatever happens between Stephen and me, it isn't your concern.'

'Isn't it?'

'No.' Olivia was adamant.

'Because I'm too young?'

Olivia sighed. 'Yes.'

'You're crazy!'

'No, I'm not.' She took a steadying breath. 'I don't know why I'm saying this, but, apart from anything else, I'm sure it hasn't missed your notice that—that I'm crippled!'

Conor gave her a bitter look. 'That's Stephen's excuse, not mine.'

'Oh, Conor!' Her head was aching with the effort of sustaining this argument. 'Just—just take me home,' she mumbled, digging her chin into the collar of her coat, and thereafter there was silence in the car.

The snow was falling more heavily now, she noticed, tipping her head back against the upholstery. It was congealing on the windscreen, forcing the wipers to work twice as hard to clear it, settling in fluffy flakes on the roadside, covering everything in a cloak of white. It was pretty, she supposed, struggling to think of anything but Conor, and the things he had been saying. It would be all too easy to give in to his persistence, all too easy to let him have his way.

But, although she was prepared to accept that he was attracted to her, she didn't believe the part he said she had played in his life. In the nine years since she'd last seen him, she doubted he'd even given her a second thought. Maybe at Christmas, and birthdays, she reflected sadly. But that was all. Then, three days ago, fate had taken a hand. She had stepped into his path, and he was flattered because he thought she'd sought him out. And maybe he was a little bored with Sharon, too, she appended, despising herself for the comfort that thought brought her. He had been looking for a diversion, and she had provided it.

It wasn't until Conor turned the car into the drive of the house on Gull Rise that Olivia realised where they were. With the snowstorm obliterating all but the most immediate surroundings of the car, she had hardly been aware that they were back in Paget. But when he braked and brought the car to a halt, she sat up in some confusion.

'This isn't the inn,' she exclaimed rather foolishly, and Conor turned to look at her with wry eyes.

'No,' he conceded, studying her unguarded face for a heart-stopping moment. Then, turning away, he thrust open his door. 'As I said, we're going to have ourselves some decent coffee.'

'They serve coffee at the Ship,' Olivia pointed out swiftly, as he walked round the car, but if he could hear her he chose to ignore her words.

'Come on,' he said, yanking open her door, his hair already flecked with snow. 'It's cold out here.'

The house, conversely, was beautifully warm, and Olivia had to admit, as Conor helped her remove her coat, that it was much nicer here than at the inn. Indeed, if it weren't for her unwelcome awareness of him, she knew she would have enjoyed familiarising herself with the old place again. As it was, she couldn't resist admiring the carpeted curve of the staircase, or running a finger over the polished mahogany of the banister as she followed Conor along the hall.

She halted in the kitchen doorway, arrested by the sight of him filling the coffee-maker with water, spooning coffee grains into a filter. He worked with an easy economy of effort, obviously well used to making his own coffee, and not at all perturbed by her interested appraisal.

Then, when the machine had been switched on, he turned and rested his hips against the drainer, his hands cupping the Formica at either side of him. 'Are you hungry?' he asked, and, realising she was staring at the spot where his shirt entered his trousers, Olivia hastily removed her gaze and shook her head.

'No. But if you——'

'I'm fine.'

His tone was clipped, and, deciding it was up to her to show him she intended to keep their association on a friendly basis, she spread her hands in an encompassing gesture. 'So,' she ventured lightly, 'who looks after this place for you? I can't believe you do all the housework yourself.'

'No.' Conor hesitated a moment, as if considering whether to answer her at all. And then he said carelessly, 'One of the local women comes in twice a week.'

'Ah.' Olivia hid her relief that it wasn't Sharon after all. 'Well, she does a wonderful job!'

'Doesn't she?' Conor was sardonic. 'Do you want a guided tour?'

'I—why, no. No, of course not.' Olivia gathered her briefly scattered composure. 'I should think I know my way around here almost as well as you do.'

'Oh, yes.' Conor removed his hands from the work-surface, and folded his arms. 'I forgot. You used to tuck me in, didn't you? How could I forget that?'

Olivia took a steadying breath. 'Please, Conor——'

'Please what?' His eyes glittered. 'Please don't say anything to embarrass you? Please don't talk about things that you'd rather ignore? Like how much you're wanting me to touch you at this moment?'

'That's not true!' Olivia was appalled that he could read something into her actions that simply wasn't there. 'If you're going to start that again, then I think I'd better go.'

'Start what again?' he asked, harshly. 'Making you look at yourself as you really are, and not as you'd like to be?'

'No.' Olivia straightened her spine, putting almost all her weight on her undamaged leg. 'I've told you how I feel about you, Conor. I'm fond of you—of course I am. How could I not be after—after——'

'—all these years?' he supplied contemptuously, and with a helpless gesture she turned back into the hall.

'If you say so,' she replied wearily, and with an angry oath he came after her.

'All right,' he said, thrusting his balled fists into his jacket pockets, and she guessed how much it had cost him to give in to her. 'All right, I won't say anything else to upset you. So—where do you want it?'

Olivia's hand sought her lips. 'What?'

'The coffee,' declared Conor, a rueful twist to his mouth. 'What else?'

Olivia expelled her breath in a rush. 'Oh.' She licked her lips. 'Well—in the kitchen, I suppose. But——' she glanced round '—would you mind if I used your bathroom first?'

'Help yourself.' Conor's tone was dry. 'I guess I don't have to tell you where it is.'

'No.' Olivia shook her head, but, although Conor went back into the kitchen to check on the coffee, all the way upstairs images of him as a baby, splashing his way through a hundred noisy bath-times, filled her head.

Of course, Conor's present bathroom bore only a passing resemblance to the one Olivia remembered. The old porcelain tub had been removed, and in its place there was a perspex-walled shower cubicle, and a modern corner bath. It had been tiled, too, and on the glass shelf above the wide hand-basin a razor and blades had taken the place of the old rubber duck Olivia remembered.

There was a damp towel, too, lying on the floor, where Conor must have dropped it and, unable to help herself, Olivia bent and picked it up. The faint aroma of the soap he had used still clung to the cloth, and with a feeling of despair she buried her face in its clammy folds.

'Liv!'

Conor's voice brought her to an unwelcome awareness of what she was doing, and she flung the towel aside almost convulsively. God, she was going out of her mind, she thought, with a tremor of self-disgust. Was she really reduced to seeking comfort from a *towel*?

'Liv!' Conor's voice was much nearer now, and she realised that by not answering him she had achieved what she had been trying to avoid: his awareness of her as a vulnerable human being. 'Liv—are you OK?'

He sounded as if he was just outside the door, and she gazed at her flushed face with frustrated eyes. If only she had brought some cosmetics with her. As it was, there was no way she could disguise the fact that she had been crying.

'Liv——'

'Yes, I'm all right.' In spite of her efforts, her voice was higher than it should be. 'I—I'll be down in a minute.'

'Well—if you're sure.'

'I'm sure.' Olivia stood on the other side of the door, praying he wouldn't ask what she was doing. She cleared her throat, and managed a lower tone. 'I'm sorry for taking so long.'

There was a silence that was almost audibly analytical, and then Conor said, 'No problem,' in a flat, unemotional tone, and she heard him move away towards the stairs.

She waited several minutes until she was sure he had had time to reach the kitchen, and then opened the door. As she had expected, the landing was deserted, and, moving silently across it, she opened the door into what had once been Sally and Keith's bedroom. She guessed it was most probably the room Conor used now, and, while the connotations of that reality caused a fluttery feeling in her stomach, her need was greater than her fears.

Besides, she consoled herself, her motives were innocent enough. Well, mostly, she conceded, as her eyes moved hungrily over the familiar appointments of the apartment. But it had occurred to her that if Sharon had *stayed*—she stumbled over the word—at the house, she might have left a lipstick behind her. Not that the idea of using anything of Sharon's was particularly appealing to her, but she was desperate.

However, as she walked across the soft oatmeal carpet, it wasn't Sharon's presence that invaded her senses. In fact, there was no evidence that Sharon had ever been in the room. It was Conor's clothes that were strewn haphazardly about the place, and Conor's towelling bathrobe draped over the rail at the foot of the unmade bed.

Her eyes flicked quickly away from the bed, but the temptation to touch his clothes was almost irresistible. Still, she overcame it, and approached the solid oak dressing-table. If Sharon had left any personal belongings behind, surely this was where they would be, and, ignoring the censure she knew she would see in her reflection, she jerked the top drawer open.

'Looking for something, Liv?'

Conor's quiet enquiry almost scared the life out of her, and she dropped the box of cuff-links she had been holding, feeling like a thief caught rifling the premises. The tiny gold and silver items spilled all over the floor, and Olivia wanted to die of embarrassment.

'I...' She dragged her eyes away from the scattered pieces and looked helplessly at him. But the need to justify herself was uppermost. 'I—wasn't being nosy.'

'Did I say you were?' Conor had been standing with his arms folded, his shoulder propped against the frame of the door, but now he straightened and came into the room. 'Not that I've got anything to hide.'

Olivia sighed, and, remembering why she had wanted something to disguise her appearance, she felt a sense of resignation. She could only hope that he would attribute her swollen eyes and bare lips to the ignominy of her position.

'I—was—just looking for a—comb,' she improvised swiftly, realising she *couldn't* admit to searching for something of Sharon's. 'I'm sorry.'

Conor glanced at the dressing-table. 'Isn't my comb good enough?' he asked drily, and, following his gaze, Olivia saw the silver-backed brushes and comb she had overlooked earlier.

Allowing her breath to escape from lungs that felt decidedly inadequate at this moment, she moved her shoulders in a helpless gesture. 'I...didn't notice them,' she mumbled lamely, averting her gaze, and Conor's hand came to lift her chin.

'Why don't you ever admit the truth, Liv?' he demanded, his thumb brushing across her stiff lips. 'You wanted to see for yourself that I wasn't lying when I said Sharon didn't live with me.'

'*No*!' His words were sufficiently outrageous to give Olivia the strength to jerk her chin from his grasp. 'You flatter yourself, Conor Brennan!' she snapped, and, grasping the corner of the dressing-table, she levered herself down on to the floor, and began gathering the scattered cuff-links together.

It wasn't the most elegant thing she had ever done. As yet, she couldn't bear her weight on her injured knee, and consequently she had to sit on the floor, with one leg tucked under her, and the other stretched out. It also meant she had to shuffle across the floor on her bottom when those nearest to her had all been collected into a small pile.

'Liv!' Conor's use of her name was exasperated, and he squatted on his haunches beside her, successfully preventing her from reaching the last few pieces. 'Liv, leave them! I'll pick them up later.'

'I can do it,' she exclaimed, aware that several tendrils of hair had come loose from the knot she had secured earlier, and were now falling into her eyes. She pushed them back with a frustrated hand as she attempted to edge past him, but the dressing-table stool was in the way, and she got herself wedged. 'Will you move?'

'Liv, listen to me...' he began, but she was no longer totally in control of her actions. She was desperate to prove she was not the helpless creature he seemed to think her, and when he reached out to grasp her hand she forcibly pushed him away.

Unfortunately, Conor was caught off balance. Squatting as he was, his weight was not evenly distributed, and when she pushed him he tried to save himself by grabbing the rail at the foot of the bed. He missed, his hand only encountering the folds of his bathrobe and bringing it down on top of him. Then, as Olivia watched with horrified eyes, he toppled back on to the floor, his head striking one of the solid black castors with a sickening thud.

'Oh, God!' Abandoning her search for the cuff-links, Olivia scrambled towards him, and for once she never even felt the protesting pain in her leg. 'Conor!' she cried, when she saw that his eyes were closed, and, reaching awkwardly across him, she fumbled for the pulse beneath his ear.

It was still there—fast and erratic, it was true, but reassuringly strong. What she would have done if it hadn't been, she didn't care to speculate. All that mattered was that he was still alive, and her hand trembled as it brushed his cheek and the bronze tips of his absurdly long lashes.

'Oh, Conor,' she breathed, and, unable to help herself, she bent her head and touched her lips to the slightly parted contours of his mouth.

CHAPTER TEN

CONOR'S response was unexpected, and instantaneous. His tongue came to meet her lips, and she found her mouth clinging to his. Almost compulsively, her fingers slid into the silky length of his hair, and the kiss deepened to a breath-robbing assault.

His eyes opened as she was drawing back, a belated sense of the impropriety of what she was doing causing her to try and rescue her composure, but his expression was frankly sensual.

'Don't go,' he said, and she felt his hand at the back of her neck. 'I may be in need of more mouth-to-mouth resuscitation.'

Olivia pressed her lips together, trying to summon some resentment towards him for frightening her like that, but she was so relieved he was all right that she could only shake her head. 'You—you're impossible,' she said unsteadily, becoming aware that he had removed his jacket while she had been using the bathroom, and he grinned.

'Whatever it takes,' he said huskily, and, drawing her mouth back to his, he rolled over until she was lying flat on her back. 'Just don't—tell me you don't want me now.'

Olivia groaned. 'But I—I'm such a mess,' she stammered, while his mouth, moving over the silken curve of her cheek, denied her protest.

'You're crazy,' he told her, threading his hands through her hair, and scattering her hairpins as she had scattered his cuff-links a few minutes ago. His thumbs smoothed the dark shadows her tears had painted beneath her eyes. 'Is that why you were crying?'

She moved her head helplessly from side to side. 'We—we shouldn't do this——'

'But we're going to,' he essayed a little roughly. His eyes lowered to where his fingers were tracing the neckline of her blouse. 'This is for us. No one else.'

Olivia's resistance was faltering. Everywhere he touched, her skin felt sensitised, and when he unbuttoned the first few buttons of her blouse and delicately stroked the tops of her breasts a wave of uncontrollable longing swept over her. Her nipples hardened beneath their lacy covering, and she knew he had noticed her reaction when his tongue circled his lips in undisguised anticipation.

Her eyes drooped beneath the hunger she could see in his. What if she disappointed him? she thought raggedly. What did she know of making love, other than the rather unsatisfactory coupling she and Stephen had indulged in? What if this turned out to be a terrible mistake? How would she live with herself if it all went wrong...?

'Look at me,' Conor said, interrupting her anxious introspection, and when her lids flickered upwards she saw he had torn open the buttons of his own shirt and dragged it out of his trousers. 'Help me,' he added, and almost automatically her hands moved to ease the shirt off his shoulders.

But, after he had discarded it on to the floor, her hands lingered on his chest, and on the fine pelt of honey-coloured hair that arrowed so enticingly down to his navel. It felt so clean—so *good*—that she wanted to bury her face in its downy softness, and she knew Stephen had never made her feel so aware of her own weakness.

Conor was unbuttoning the rest of her blouse now, and his fingers made short work of the front fastening on her bra. Experience, she supposed, as a fleeting surge of uncontrolled jealousy swept over her, but then he bent his head to her breasts and all negative emotion was cast aside.

She caught her breath as he licked the sensitive peak of one breast, and when his teeth fastened round the nipple and tugged, ever so gently, her heart nearly exploded.

'Beautiful,' he breathed, his hand running possessively down her body to her thigh, before returning to ease both her blouse and the chunky cardigan from her shoulders. 'But now, I want to see you naked.'

Olivia stiffened. Until then, she had been so wrapped up in what he was doing to her body that she hadn't given a thought to how she would feel about him seeing her totally nude. It was all very well—if a little exaggerated—for him to say she was beautiful, when his attention was concentrated on the slender curve of her torso. But how would he feel—how would *she* feel— when he peeled off her leggings, and...?

But she couldn't go any further. 'I—can't,' she got out miserably, suddenly aware of the texture of the carpet at her back, the incongruity of making love on the floor when there was a perfectly good bed just a few feet away. 'You don't understand...'

Conor's eyes were so dark a green that she felt as if she were drowning in their shaded depths. 'What don't I understand precisely?' he asked, one leg wedged between her knees, and a finger lightly probing the waistband of her leggings. The timbre of his voice lowered. 'Do you really think I don't know what you're afraid of?'

Olivia moved her head. 'You don't know what I look like,' she insisted, and Conor sighed.

'Then let's see, shall we?' he suggested evenly, and, ignoring her outraged hands, he dragged the leggings down over her hips.

The fact that her silk knickers were tugged away along with the leggings didn't immediately register. She was so shocked at the high-handed way he had acted that she could only lie there with her eyes closed, as a wave of hot embarrassment swept over her. Only it wasn't just embarrassment, she acknowledged painfully. It was shame, and humiliation, and downright anger. How could he have done such a thing? Without even the protection of a sheet to hide her blushes?

And then, like a balm to her mortified flesh, she felt his mouth moving on her thigh. His lips were following the line of the ugly scar that seared from her groin to her knee, she realised incredulously. He was kissing her, soothing her quivering limb with sensuous caresses that burned their way into her consciousness, and left her weak and helpless.

Her eyes opened, shifting quickly from the high ceiling to the amazing sight of Conor's bent head. The snowstorm was over, and the clear light from a white world filled the room with brilliance. It silvered Conor's hair, showing up the darkness of the strands the snow had dampened earlier, and as he sensed her gaze and lifted his head a silky wave fell against his temple.

Olivia moved then, her hand lifting to touch his hair before sliding to the nape of his neck. But Conor captured her fingers in passing, drawing her palm against his mouth. Then, with his eyes still on her, he allowed his tongue to caress her palm, causing the drenching heat of excitement to pool between her legs.

Olivia was shaking with emotion when he knelt and lifted her into his arms. Then, lowering his mouth to hers, he got to his feet, and walked the short distance to the bed.

The sheets were cool, but oh, so soft against her bare shoulders, and he only paused long enough to strip off his trousers before sliding on to the bed beside her.

'Better?' he breathed huskily, spreading her hair out on the pillow, and burying his face in its dusky tangle, and she could only nod bemusedly. But the world had narrowed to this room, this bed, and this man, and for the first time in their association she was prepared to let him have his way.

His tongue slid into her mouth, filling her with the taste and the feel of him, hot and wet, and devastatingly real. Against her breasts, the hair-roughened skin of his chest was unbearably erotic. When he rolled to one side to explore her hips and her navel and the sensitive inner curve of her thigh, she looked down and saw the glistening shaft of his manhood rearing from its nest of darker blond hair.

Her nails dug into her palms as the emotions the mere sight of his arousal evoked inside her threatened to overwhelm her, and then, unable to stop herself, she uncurled her fingers and let them seek their own destiny. The hot velvety skin swelled beneath her touch, and with a groan that was half pain, half ecstasy, Conor slid over her.

'Don't—don't do that,' he implored her brokenly, and then, seeing her instinctive withdrawal, he drew her hand back to his body. 'All right, do it,' he conceded. 'Just don't expect my control to be limitless.'

Olivia licked her lips. 'What control?' she asked, relaxing, and Conor's mouth cut off the soft smile of understanding that tugged at her lips.

Her head swam as his weight pressed her into the mattress, and her legs parted to admit his probing hand. His fingers slid between the moist curls, seeking the slick cleft that was already throbbing in anticipation, and when he stroked the sensitive nub of her femininity she could barely suppress the urge to thrust herself against him.

'Good,' he whispered, the unsteadiness of his voice revealing his own dwindling self-control, and, instead of answering, she wound her arms around his neck.

It was all an exquisite agony, a soul-wrenching torture that demanded its own fulfilment. She had never felt this way with Stephen, never felt this way before, and the need for him to invade her body was becoming an unbearable torment.

She found herself moving against him, rotating her hips, inviting his participation, showing him without words exactly how she felt. Her mouth was swollen, bruised by the hungry possession of his mouth, but it was another possession entirely that she wanted now.

And Conor had driven himself beyond the point of rationality. With movements that were motivated purely by instinct, he guided himself to the very threshold of her womanhood and then, with an aching need that Olivia's body echoed, he buried himself in her yielding flesh.

'Oh, God,' he groaned, as her muscles expanded to admit him and then closed tightly about him. 'God, Liv—I'm going to make a mess of this.'

'Sh-sh,' she whispered, content for the moment just to enjoy the sensation of him stretching her and filling her in a way she had never experienced before. Acting purely on impulse, she lifted her legs to facilitate his moving even deeper inside her, and a moan of frustration broke from him.

'Aw—hell!' he swore, and, feeling the sudden hot flood of his release, Olivia guessed what had happened.

'It's all right,' she breathed, hanging on to his shoulders when he would have dragged himself away. 'I don't mind, honestly.' And, in spite of her own unrequited needs, it was true. She had wanted to please him and she had. And that was what mattered.

'I mind,' he muttered, some minutes later, when the shuddering spasm of his climax had left his body. He levered himself up on to his elbows, placed at either side of her head. 'I wanted this to be perfect. Instead of which, I lost control like a demented schoolboy!'

'Well, you were,' she said softly, smoothing the damp hair back from his forehead with teasing hands, and he frowned.

'I was what?'

'Demented,' she told him gently, and, guessing he thought she had meant something else, she added, 'But nothing like a schoolboy.'

'And I didn't wear anything,' he declared, turning his lips against her fingers. 'After all the advice I've given my patients on the need to use a condom, and when you touched me I couldn't wait long enough to put one on.'

Olivia took a quivering breath. 'Do you wish you had?' she asked, and Conor gave her a rueful look.

'No,' he said huskily, lowering his forehead until it was resting against hers. 'It's you I'm concerned about, not me.'

'Well, don't be,' she whispered, guessing he would assume she was using some other form of protection. She stroked his mouth with her finger. 'Did I—did you—was it all right?'

His expression was tender. 'You are joking?'

Olivia caught her lower lip between her teeth. 'I just thought——'

'Liv, I've wanted you here, in my bed, for longer than I can remember. And since that morning you practically collapsed on my doorstep I've thought of nothing else but you.' He used his thumbs to massage her temples, as his lips and his tongue caressed her willing mouth. 'How do you think it feels to know I'm a part of you? I could live forever and never top the magic of this moment.'

'Oh, Conor...'

Her breathless cry was against his lips, and her arms closed convulsively around his neck. She was very much afraid she would never know such happiness again, and the prospect of him leaving her made every second precious.

The growing awareness of his arousal caused her hold on him to falter. She hadn't known a man could become aroused again so quickly, and Conor's eyes, as she pressed him away from her, were faintly rueful.

'Yes,' he said softly, taking one of her quivering hands and drawing it down to where their bodies were joined. 'Did you honestly think it was over? God, Liv, we could stay here all day and night as well and I'd still want more.'

Olivia's eyes were wide and luminous. 'You—you don't have to say that,' she protested, and Conor's lips twisted.

'Oh, yes, I do,' he averred huskily, pushing her back against the pillows, and the possession of his mouth left her no room for doubts.

And nothing had prepared her for the way she would feel when Conor began to move inside her. The sensations she felt when his powerful body slid in and out of hers filled her with a spiralling kind of torment. They taught her that what she and Stephen had shared had had no force, no substance, and how could she hope to assuage a hunger that had never been slaked?

But as Conor cupped her buttocks so that he could penetrate to the very core of her being, the flame he had ignited began to engulf her. His urgent body thrust ever more forcefully into hers, and every straining muscle brought an answering response that was purely physical. Her mind might be torturing her with her lack of experience, but her body knew exactly what it wanted.

Hardly aware of what she was doing, she clutched Conor's neck, her nails digging into his flesh, and she dragged his mouth back to hers. Now, her tongue invaded his mouth, sucking his lips, crushing herself against him, so that from breast to thigh there were fused together by the sweat of their bodies.

'God, Liv,' he groaned, ramming himself into her, and the raging fire in her blood melted the final restraints inside her. With a choking sob, she reached the precipice and plunged eagerly over the edge, spilling out into a space so incredibly beautiful that she could feel the hot tears of gratitude running helplessly down her cheeks. Seconds later, Conor joined her, the rushing warmth of his seed sending her into another involuntary convulsion, so that it was some time before either of them was capable of coherent thought...

Predictably, it was Conor who eventually broke their embrace. Realising he was probably crushing her beneath the weight of his powerful body, he rolled with evident reluctance on to his back, shielding his eyes from the glare outside with a lazy arm.

Then, expelling his breath on a contented sigh, he rolled on to his side. Propping himself on one elbow, he looked down at her, and it said something for Olivia's state of mind that she didn't immediately rush to drag the covers over her.

'I love you,' he said, his green eyes dark and intent. 'And I want you to divorce Stephen, and marry me.'

Olivia blinked, and then, when his hand came to rub the treacherous tears from her cheeks, she struggled to summon all the objections that had been so obvious in her before he robbed her of all intelligent thought.

But lying there, looking up into his soulful gaze, it was difficult to think of anything but the singular delight it would be if he were to make love to her again. Having once tasted heaven, she could quite see why someone would want to taste it again, though in Conor's case her involvement was probably not essential.

'Are you listening to me?' he demanded now, his hand drifting down over her throat, lingering momentarily at the helpless arousal of her breast, before continuing on to the cluster of dark curls that guarded her womanhood. He bent his head to touch her there, and then, his voice thickening, he added, 'Don't tell me you still love him, because I don't believe you.'

Olivia felt her legs parting under that deliberate stimulation, and it was a distinct effort to press them together. But, in doing so, she trapped his fingers, and she reached down to remove his hand with scarcely concealed anguish.

'No,' she said, groping for the sheet that was crumpled beneath them. His weight was on it, and she tugged ineffectually. 'Please!'

'Please, what?' he said, half annoyed by her obvious efforts to dislodge him, and Olivia rolled on to her side away from him.

'I—I have to go,' she said, and with an impatient oath Conor dragged the sheet out from underneath him, and tossed it over her.

'If you're so desperate to hide yourself—here,' he said, shifting on to his back again. 'But for God's sake, Liv, stop kidding yourself that what's just happened is going to go away.'

'It has to,' she said, in a muffled voice, knowing she should get off the bed, but incapable right then of doing so. 'Conor, I—I'm not saying that—that I don't care for you——'

'Oh, thanks!'

'—but you and me—we're no good together.'

Conor swore. 'Don't be stupid!' His hand reached for her shoulder, turning her on to her back again. He rolled to face her, his eyes dark with a mixture of both passion and anger. 'After what we've just shared, you can still say——'

'It's not enough,' insisted Olivia painfully, the words she was trying to say tearing her apart. 'Conor, what we just had was—was sex; plain and simple. Not something on which to build a lifetime's commitment; not when there are so many other reasons why we'd fail.'

Conor scowled. 'Tell me, then. Tell me these reasons. I've told you I care about you, and I'm pretty sure you care about me. That's not sex talking, Liv. That's love!'

The urge to give in, to tell him she agreed with him, that she'd do anything he wanted, as long as they could stay together, was almost unbearable. How could she turn him away? How could she deny what they had undeniably had? Was anything worse than the trauma of never seeing him again? For if she left him now, that was what it meant. She couldn't do it any other way.

But the habits of a lifetime were hard to break, and she was simply not able to justify that kind of weakness, even to herself. She had to end it now, before his persistence and her own need undermined her reason. At least she had known how it could be with someone you loved. Some women went through their whole lives without experiencing perfection.

'I'm—too old for you,' she began, knowing what he would say, and prepared for it this time. 'Conor, you're young, you're ambitious, you've got your whole life in front of you. I would only hold you back. You know it, and I know it. Besides, I—still have a husband.' She crossed her fingers on the lie. 'And he's not likely to divorce me if he thinks that you're involved'

'Then I'll wait,' said Conor flatly. 'Sooner or later, he's got to give in.'

'No——'

'Yes.' He closed his eyes against the denial he could see in her face. 'Liv, I don't care how long it takes. I've waited eleven years already.'

Olivia let her breath out rather unevenly. 'So you say.'

'So I know.' His eyes flicked open. 'What do I have to do to make you believe me? What's five years more or less in a lifetime?'

'It's the difference between me being thirty-four and nearly forty,' retorted Olivia harshly. 'Conor, when you get married, you'll want children. I don't even know if I can have any. I—I haven't had any luck so far. And—and before you ask, I—might have done.'

Conor's expression was grim. 'And if I say that I don't care whether or not you can perpetuate the Brennan dynasty?'

Olivia sighed. 'I care,' she said steadily. 'And—and your mother would care, if she were still alive.'

Conor stared at her for another heart-stopping moment, and she had the feeling that if he touched her now her defences would crumble like the pathetic things they were. But then an expression of bitterness filled his face, and without another word he got up from the bed.

He paused when he reached the bedroom door, however, turning back to look at her, heartbreakingly appealing in his naked masculinity. 'My mother would never have stopped us, you know,' he said, his eyes dark with pain. 'But if that's the only excuse you've got to offer, then I guess I did get the wrong message.'

Olivia closed her eyes against the subtle accusation of his words, and when she opened them again he was gone. A few moments later, she heard the sound of water running, and as she dragged herself off the bed she guessed he was taking a shower.

She wanted to go to him even then. She knew the bathroom door wouldn't be locked, that he would be hoping, even now, that she would change her mind. All she had to do was open the door, step into the shower cubicle with him, and let the future take care of itself. She could do it. She wasn't married, even if he still thought she was. She had nothing to be ashamed of.

But it was the fear of his ultimate rejection that made her turn aside from such temptation. The fear that she would last no longer than Sharon, or any of the other women he had known since he left England ten years ago. And, strangely enough, she knew he could hurt her far more than Stephen had ever done. And she had had too much pain already.

Besides, she argued, she had her career to consider. She wasn't like Sharon. She had never allowed any man to come between her and the people she had been trained to defend. In that, she conceded, Stephen had been right. She had had too little time for him. So why should it be any different with Conor? She wasn't the emotional type.

Only she was. *She was*. Standing there, staring at her reflection in the long cheval-mirror, she acknowledged that what had been wrong with her marriage to Stephen was that she simply hadn't loved him enough. But, until now, she had had nothing to measure it against. Now she had. Crazy as it sounded, she was falling *in love* with Conor.

But she couldn't. As her fingers probed the bruises his lovemaking had left on her body, she knew she had to start thinking with her mind again, instead of her senses. It would be too easy to give in to the insidious attraction he had for her, too easy to forget that she already had one failed marriage behind her, and that she had sworn when she divorced Stephen that she would never get herself into that situation again.

Of course, that was before she had met Conor again, she admitted, before she had realised that the love she had had for him when they were children could mature into something infinitely more powerful. Which was just another reason why she couldn't let it go on. If she had been younger, fitter, maybe they would have stood a chance. As it was, she would be fooling herself if she thought this relationship could bring her anything but more heartache. And of a much more devastating kind...

She suddenly realised that the water had stopped running, and, aware that Conor would come back at any second, she hurriedly scrambled into her clothes. She was buttoning her blouse when he came back into the room, and she averted her eyes as he crossed the room to take clean underwear from the dressing-table drawer.

'You could have had a shower, too,' he observed, and she was shaken by the absence of feeling in his voice. It was as if their relationship had never progressed beyond the point of bare civility, and she turned to look at him with unguarded eyes.

But then, realising she was in danger of revealing exactly what his attitude meant to her, she groped for her cardigan. 'I—I'll have one later,' she stammered, fumbling her arms into sleeves that were turned inside out. She moved to the window. 'Um—at least it's stopped snowing.'

'Has it?' Conor's tone hadn't changed, but the contempt in his face was shrivelling. 'You know, I hadn't noticed.'

Olivia bit her lower lip. 'I—don't be like this,' she implored, and for a moment she glimpsed the anguish he was trying so hard to conceal.

'I thought this was what you wanted,' he replied, and her nails dug into her palms as he pulled a navy polo shirt over his head. It was probably the last time she would share such an intimacy with him, and her heart ached at the futility of what she was doing.

But, 'Yes. Yes, it is,' she mumbled, and, even though it was tearing her to pieces, she met his accusing gaze with calm determination. She limped heavily to the door. 'Will you take me home?'

CHAPTER ELEVEN

THREE months later, on a perfect day in late spring, Olivia stood beside Stephen's widowed mother, as his coffin was lowered into the ground. The older woman was crying, stifling her sobs in the handkerchief she had pressed to her face. And, although Olivia was less affected by her surroundings, she, too, could feel the tightness of grief gripping her throat.

But it was all so unbelievable, she thought. That Stephen should actually be dead! That they should be burying a man who would have only been forty-five on his next birthday. It seemed so unfair.

Not that his death had been the act of revenge she had at first imagined. When Mrs Perry had rung in tears, begging her to come and comfort her, Olivia had instantly thought of Harry Darcy, and Stephen's fears when he had come to the inn in Paget. In spite of the pain even thinking of those days evoked in her, she had briefly wondered if Harry had found out about Stephen's affair with his wife, and carried out his threat.

But, to her considerable relief, she had discovered that that was not the case. Although it had evidently been difficult for his mother to admit, she had eventually confessed that Stephen had breathed his last in another woman's arms. A married woman, it was true, but not Karen Darcy. Her son had died, as he had lived, without giving any thought to the consequences of his actions.

Which was why it was left to Olivia to make all the arrangements for his funeral. Mrs Perry was too distressed to do it for herself, and, until her sister arrived from Manchester, Olivia had borne the whole burden of her tears and recriminations.

She hadn't blamed Olivia, exactly. But she had made it known that she considered Olivia was responsible for the divorce. No *reasonable* woman expected a man to be totally faithful, she said. Which had made Olivia wonder about the kind of life Mrs Perry had led with Stephen's father. Like his son, Mr Perry had died of a heart attack in middle age.

In any event, by the day of the funeral Olivia was quite relieved to hand over the reins to Mrs Perry's sister. She had been glad to help, but it had become something of a strain. Her own life was not without its complications, but it was not something she could confide in Stephen's mother.

Harry Darcy approached her as they were leaving the cemetery. As Stephen's employer, he had naturally attended the service, and his swarthy features were kind and sympathetic.

'Well, Olivia,' he said, 'this is a tragedy. Particularly as Steve had told me that you and he might be getting back together again. What can I say?'

Olivia's gaze flickered over the face of the willowy blonde clinging to Harry's sleeve. Karen Darcy looked nervous. And why not? thought Olivia drily. Stephen was dead, but Olivia wasn't, and she must know he had confided in his ex-wife. And, for all his faults, Stephen had paid a high price for his indiscretions. Why should Karen escape scot-free?

But, with a mental shrug of her shoulders, Olivia accepted Harry's condolences without controversy. She neither confirmed nor denied the comment he had made about their relationship, but that didn't matter. And after all, there was nothing to be gained by hurting Karen now. She only hoped the younger woman had learned her lesson.

Though, as she watched them walk away together, Olivia somehow doubted it. Now that the burden of guilt had been lifted from her shoulders, there was a definite spring in Karen's step.

Lucky Karen, thought Olivia later that afternoon, as she said goodbye to Mrs Perry and her sister, and got behind the wheel of her small saloon to drive home. If only her own problems could be dealt with so carelessly. If only she had someone to solve them for her.

And it had seemed simple enough when she left Paget. By putting the best part of a hundred miles between her and Conor, she had proved she had the strength to do it. And, with her work, and the friends who hadn't deserted her after the divorce, she had been determined to forget all about him.

Of course, the events of that snowy morning had altered her plans. The idea of continuing her holiday had been quickly cast aside. All she had wanted to do was go to ground, preferably in familiar surroundings. Even the thought that Stephen might pester her if she went back home had seemed infinitely preferable to risking seeing Conor again.

Looking back now, she realised what she had really been doing was running from herself. Her fears of seeing Conor, the urgency she had felt to immerse herself in familiar things, had been her way of blinding herself to the truth. When she had boarded the train to London, the relief she'd felt had been just an illusion. And, like all illusions, it had eventually evaporated.

The dreams had come first, invading her sleep with images, not of herself and Conor, but of Conor with some other woman. Sometimes it was Sharon, and those images were bad enough. But, later, it was someone else, someone Olivia didn't know, and they were the worst of all.

So, she slept badly, and awakened drained of all energy. Her cosy apartment, which had previously been such a welcome haven, began to stifle her. Insidiously, the pain had surfaced, subconsciously at first, and then sharply real. It made a nonsense of the unhappiness she had felt over Stephen's deception. Her need for Conor was like a living disease, feeding on her flesh.

She started going out then, trailing round the shops for hours, desperate for diversion. She even joined a health club, and spent long hours exhausting herself in the swimming-pool. Her leg strengthened, and, because her appetite improved, she put on a little weight. But while her body mended, her brain corroded, and she knew something had to be done to retain her sanity.

She went back to the office the following week. Mr Halliday was endearingly pleased to see her, even if he did wonder whether she ought not to have given herself a little more time before returning to work. But her apparent eagerness, and the air of confidence she managed to convey, convinced him she knew what she was doing. And, to her relief, she discovered that at that level she could still function fairly normally.

And, gradually, the madness had subsided. She was even able to question her feeling of devastation when Conor hadn't so much as picked up a phone to assure himself that she'd got home safely. And he might have done. Once he'd got over his pique. It wasn't as if she'd been wiped off the face of the earth. His protestations of undying love must have melted along with the snow.

That the manner of her leaving had not been entirely unselfish was something she preferred not to dwell on. That Conor might have had some justification for his anger was best set aside. If her own fears of rejection had worked against her, she chose not to recognise the fact. And even when something happened to mitigate the pain, she refused to consider the consequences.

Stephen's death had come at a time when she was trying not to think about the future. And, selfish as it sounded, it had given her a breathing space. For a time, someone else's needs had taken precedence, and she had submerged her own problems in theirs. But it was over now. She had to get on with her own life.

Letting herself into her apartment, she looked about her with rueful eyes. For the past seventy-two hours she had been at Mrs Perry's beck and call, and her neglect of this place showed. There were crumbs on the floor, and dishes in the sink, and her bed hadn't been made in days. She had come home to sleep and little else. Even the light on the answerphone was blinking.

Well, it would have to wait, she decided. Everything would have to wait. She needed a shower and something to eat, not necessarily in that order.

Fifteen minutes later she came out of the bathroom with a towel tucked sarong-wise under her arms. She had washed her hair, too, and she paused in front of the dressing-table to towel it dry. As she did so, the sarong slipped away, and she was left with the disturbing reflection of her own naked body.

Her hands stilled, and, lowering her arms to her sides, she stared at herself with troubled eyes. Was it visible yet? she wondered. She turned sideways. Yes, barely. Just the slightest thickening at her waist giving her condition away.

Swallowing, she bent and lifted the bath towel again. Then, wrapping it tightly about her, she turned away from the mirror. Sooner or later, she was going to have to make a decision, she realised tensely. No matter how unattractive the prospect might be, the choice had to be made.

Beyond her windows, the trees in the park were burgeoning with new life, and she stood for several minutes staring at them before her growling stomach drove her into the kitchen. She was burgeoning with new life, too, she thought ruefully, as she prepared herself a peanut butter sandwich. And, whatever happened, it was a cause for rejoicing, not regret.

Carrying her sandwich back into the living-room, she perched on the arm of her sofa and pressed the rewind button on the answerphone. It was the dilemma of how— or if—she should tell Conor that was causing her so much heart-searching, and as she munched on her sandwich she had to acknowledge she was no closer to a decision now than she had been before Stephen's untimely death.

The trouble was, she had no way of knowing how he might react to the news that he was going to be a father. If, as she expected, he had got over his infatuation for her, he would certainly not welcome such daunting news. Oh, she was sure he wouldn't abjure his responsibilities. He was an honourable man, and he would respect her wishes. But did she really want to tie him to her, on any terms? And particularly like this, the oldest trick in the book.

In all honesty, it would be easier to keep it from him, and she guessed that after learning that Stephen had spent the night at the inn in Paget her friends would assume the child was his. She could handle it that way if she wanted.

But, deep inside her, she had a powerful need to tell Conor the truth. That was the real dilemma. She wanted him to know she was having his baby. She wanted him to share in the wonder.

What wonder? she thought now, crossly, as the rewind button clicked off, and the first recorded message was replayed. Taking another mouthful of her sandwich, she listened as a colleague from work informed her that one of her clients, presently on bail, had absconded. The man was believed to have fled to Ireland, but Olivia couldn't summon any real irritation at the news. Ever since she had discovered she was pregnant, her focus had altered completely, and she had to force herself to consider the case with some degree of subjectivity.

The next voice was not immediately familiar to her, and, switching off the machine, she went to get herself a can of juice from the fridge. She couldn't drink coffee any more without feeling nauseous, and it was this as much as anything that had first alerted her to her condition. She had never actually suffered from morning sickness. But the scent of freshly brewed coffee was definitely taboo.

She carried the can back into the living-room, and resumed her position beside the phone. Depressing the button on the recorder, she re-started the next message, tackling the ring-pull on the can as she did so. Unfortunately, the can must have been shaken, because the juice fizzed out all over the towel, and she was muttering to herself as she went to get some paper towels from the kitchen when the identity of her caller hit her. It was Mrs Drake, calling from Paget. And, although Conor's name hadn't been mentioned, Olivia abandoned the can and hurried back to re-wind the tape.

'Mrs Perry? Mrs Perry, are you there?' Olivia caught her upper lip between her teeth as her erstwhile landlady's voice betrayed her uncertainty. Then, 'Oh, it's one of those awful machines,' she said, and for a few seconds there was silence. But, eventually, she overcame her reticence and went on, 'Mrs Perry, this is Eva Drake calling. From the Ship. That's the Ship Inn, in Paget,' she added, bringing a faint smile to Olivia's strained face. 'You remember?' You stayed with us a few months ago.'

How could she forget? Olivia contained her impatience, and the woman continued, 'I'm calling about a personal matter, Mrs Perry. I hope you won't think I'm poking my nose in where it's not wanted, but after I'd spoken to Connie, well...'

She broke off again, and Olivia wanted to scream. If she wasn't careful, the woman was going to run out of tape. And she had the feeling Mrs Drake wouldn't ring again.

'You remember Connie, don't you, Mrs Perry? She said she met you one day at the clinic. Connie Holmes, that is. Sharon's mother.'

Yes, yes, go on, Olivia implored silently, and to her relief she did.

'Of course, I didn't tell Connie I might ring you, Mrs Perry. Even now, I'm not sure I'm doing the right thing. But your husband did say you'd known the family for a long time. And when I heard about poor Dr Brennan——'

Conor! What about Conor?

'—I thought maybe you'd want to know.'

To know what?

Olivia was almost beside herself with frustration now. Hurry up, Mrs Drake, she begged. What's happened to Conor?

'It seems there was an—accident at the clinic,' the woman faltered, the doubt in her voice growing stronger. Olivia was half afraid she was going to ring off without finishing the call. 'Course, you may know this already, but when Connie said Sharon had lost patience with him, and that he was letting nobody into that house to help him, I had to do something. That's my nature, Mrs Perry. I like to help people.'

Thank God for that, thought Olivia weakly, wishing she had felt more charitably towards her while she was there. But there was still so much she hadn't explained.

'Anyway,' Mrs Drake was saying now, and it was obvious she was preparing to hang up, 'I've done my duty. If—if Dr Brennan had some family, it would be different. But he doesn't. He's got nobody, Mrs Perry. And—I just thought that you—well, you'll know what I mean,' she finished, and the line went dead.

An hour and a half later, Olivia was driving along the M20 heading for Folkestone. It was already seven o'clock, and she would have been further had it not been for the rush-hour traffic in London. Her apartment was fairly central, and getting out of the city on a Friday evening was never easy. Apart from the usual log-jam of cars that used the motorways every evening, there were the weekend trippers, heading for coast and country with a total disregard for serious travellers. To drive in London at all you had to have nerves of steel, and Olivia thought it said much for her concern for Conor that she hadn't flinched at joining the queues.

But the awful memories of her accident were now behind her, thank goodness. These past months of physical activity had helped enormously. She still dragged her left leg a little, particularly if she was tired, but even the scars were fading now that she was gaining weight.

It was ironic, really, she thought. She had been going through one of the most traumatic periods of her life, and she had put weight on. Thank heavens for small mercies, she mused, running a possessive hand over the slight swelling beneath her waistband. This baby had saved her life. Perhaps it would save Conor's, too.

But such thoughts were futile. She had no real idea what was wrong with Conor. Mrs Drake had said there had been an accident at the clinic, but that could mean anything. And had the fact that Sharon had rejected him had anything to do with it?

Her brain buzzed with possibilities, and for once she wished she had a car-phone. She had tried to ring Mrs Drake for more details before she left the apartment, but the line was engaged. And she had been so desperate to get on her way that she had given up trying.

At least she wasn't feeling sleepy. The shower she'd had earlier had refreshed her, and hearing what Mrs Drake had had to say had proved a powerful stimulant. Now, responding to the urgency building inside her, she pressed her foot harder on the accelerator.

But luck was with her. She cruised past the turn-offs for Maidstone and Ashford without even dropping below seventy. It was only when she left the motorway that she was compelled to lower her speed, and she managed to contain her impatience all the way to Paget.

Thankfully, it was still light as she drove along the coast road. And, glancing at the sun sinking in the west, she reflected what an eventful day it had proved. First Stephen's funeral, and that pathetic little encounter with the Darcys; then her own ambivalence over telling Conor about the baby, Mrs Drake's message, and the anxiety that had sent her dashing here—and it wasn't over yet.

She hesitated when she reached the harbour, wondering if she ought to speak to Mrs Drake before driving up to Conor's house. But the car park at the inn was

full, and the prospect of going into the pub and encountering so many curious eyes deterred her. She would
thank Mrs Drake for her call—but later. Probably when
she returned to request a room for the night, she considered ruefully. Until she had spoken to Conor, she had
no idea how he would react to seeing her again.

She seemed to reach Gull Rise very quickly, and she
realised that now she was here she was no longer so convinced of the wisdom of what she was doing. Indeed, it
seemed almost presumptuous to believe that she might
succeed where others had failed. After all, Conor had
nothing to thank her for, and he could quite legitimately
refuse to speak to her.

She brought the car to a halt in front of the house.
Although the drive was empty, she didn't have the nerve
to park there, and she sat for several moments just
looking up at the windows. The curtains in Conor's
bedroom were drawn, and she wondered if that meant
he had already retired for the night. Perhaps they hadn't
been opened, she mused, remembering the state of her
own bedroom. If what Mrs Drake had said was true, it
seemed unlikely that he would regard making his bed as
a high priority.

She gnawed on her lower lip, mentally rehearsing how
she was going to explain her arrival. 'Oh, hello, Conor!
Long time no see!' No, that was no good. She frowned.
'Hi! I was in the neighbourhood, and I just thought I'd
look you up!' That was no good either. All right, then.
'Hello, Conor. Guess what? You're going to be a father!'
God, no!

She sighed. So what was she going to say? How could
she explain her appearance without involving Mrs Drake?
He would never believe she had been actually pondering
the advisability of coming here of her own free will. It
was too convenient. Too coincidental.

If she'd been secretly hoping that Conor might see the
car and come to investigate, she was disappointed. Even
though it was a good five minutes since she had turned

off the engine, the house remained as anonymous as ever.
In fact, if Mrs Drake hadn't said that he was holed up
in the house, she'd have assumed he was away. Thank
heavens for Mrs Drake, she thought uneasily, not at all
sure she really meant it. What if Conor sent her away?
What would she do then?

Pushing open her door, she put such thoughts to the
back of her mind. They were defeatist, and negative.
She was not going to consider what might, or might not,
happen. Not until she had spoken to Conor and gauged
his mood.

She shut the car and locked it, aware that she was
taking her time, delaying the moment when she had to
walk up the drive and ring the bell. But eventually she
had to approach the door, and as she mounted the steps
she thought how much easier they were for her to climb
now. Three months had made an enormous difference.
Not least in her feelings about herself.

There was no sound when she pressed the button, but
it was a large house, and she couldn't remember whether
she used to be able to hear the bell or not. However,
after several abortive attempts, she resorted to knocking,
bruising her knuckles against the panels without
achieving any more success.

'Damn,' she said aloud, glancing around. Could
Conor really not hear her? Or wasn't he answering the
door to anyone?

She could see into the drawing-room through the wide
bay, but there was no sign of life. In fact, the room had
a definite air of neglect, and the anxiety that had tor-
mented her all the way from London increased its grip.
Where was Conor? Why didn't he answer the door?

The last resort was shouting through the letter-box,
and, hoping that the one or two tenants still working in
their gardens wouldn't come to investigate, she did just
that. But, although she called his name and identified
herself, the result was the same. The house remained

unnervingly silent, and her anxiety gave way to an ominous feeling of foreboding.

She sighed. What now? She had to do something. She had to get into the house. But the idea of seeking official assistance to achieve her ends was simply not practical. It wasn't as if she was a relative or anything. The police would probably tell her to go away and mind her own business.

But she couldn't do that. In spite of a growing conviction that Conor wouldn't want to see her, she couldn't go away without assuring herself that he was all right. If only she knew what had happened. If only she knew the sequence of events. The only person who might be able to tell her was Sharon herself, and she didn't even know where she lived.

Of course, Mrs Drake would know Sharon's address. Mrs Drake probably knew more than she had said. But Mrs Drake wasn't here. And if there was nothing wrong Conor wouldn't thank her for being a scaremonger.

So, she had to find some way of getting into the house herself. She could always break a window, she mused recklessly, while the practical side of her nature threw up its hands at her audacity. But not at the front, she appended. Besides, these windows were too big.

A footpath ran between the wall of the house and the garage, and, walking along it, Olivia found herself in the back garden. There was a crumbling post, covered in honeysuckle, clinging to the rear wall of the garage, and she remembered that in Sally's day there had been a latticed gate here to keep the infant Conor from straying out on to the road. The gate was gone now, but the garden was amazingly familiar, and she paused for a moment as a whole host of memories surged over her. But then the reason she was here swept them away, and she turned her attention to the back of the house.

And, as she did so, another memory surfaced. Years ago, long before the Brennans had taken possession of the house, there had been a coke boiler in the cellar. In those days, the fuel had been delivered in sacks, and tipped, by means of a trapdoor, into the cellar. Of course, the boiler had been defunct before the Brennans moved in, and Keith had cleaned out the cellar, and used it for storage purposes. But the trapdoor must still be there.

And it was. Hidden beneath a trough of flowering shrubs, it was securely padlocked, as always, but surely offering her best chance of getting into the house. She knew the cellar. She and Conor had played there. And the door into the house had never been locked.

Breaking the padlock presented the most immediate problem, but a rummage among a pile of plant pots and canes turned up a metal tube, which looked as if it had once been part of the bicycle Conor used to ride. No wonder thieves had such a cosy time of it, she reflected, as the padlock broke at the third attempt. A little local knowledge, and the rest was easy.

The trapdoor was stiff, but it opened, and Olivia found herself gazing down at an old step-ladder, which someone had left propped against the trapdoor. 'Bingo,' she breathed, getting to her feet and starting down it. She didn't want to give herself time to have second thoughts.

The cellar was still a store-room. Olivia was glad of the light from the open trapdoor, as she stumbled over old rolled-up carpets and abandoned suitcases. Keith's wine-rack was still there, though the bottles she could see were of a more modern vintage. And there was Sally's old sewing-machine, and the tailor's dummy, which briefly gave her quite a shock.

But at last she was standing at the foot of the steps that led up into the house. The last hurdle, she thought, regarding the door at the top of the steps with some uncertainty. It was such a heavy door. What if it was locked?

At first when she turned the handle, she thought it was. It didn't open at the first attempt, and her heart sank. But, as anxiety gave way to frustration, her frenzied tugging bore fruit. It was just stiff through lack of use, and with a concerted effort she brought it swinging back against her. It nearly flattened her against the wall, but she managed to save herself, inching her way around the door and into the hall of the house.

So far so good. Closing the door behind her, Olivia rubbed her slightly grubby palms down the seams of her jeans. Now all she had to do was find Conor. If he was here...

The air felt musty, as if it was too long since anyone had opened a window. And there was a curious smell, too. She couldn't immediately identify it, but it was sweet and cloying. She frowned. Dear God, what had been going on here?

The kitchen and dining-room were as deserted as the drawing-room. There weren't even any dirty dishes in the sink, she noticed. Only a cup on the drainer, bearing dregs of what appeared to be coffee. So, Conor had to be upstairs. In bed? Remembering the closed bedroom curtains, she knew a moment's hesitation. What made her think he would be any more pleased to see her than Sharon? Particularly as she had virtually broken in. What price her legal training now?

But she had to see him. She had to know if his feelings for her had changed. If they had, then she would have to live with it. But she had to hear it from his lips. And if, by some miracle, they hadn't...

She went no further. Instead, she started up the stairs, aware that she had no real idea what she would find. It occurred to her that what she had smelt could be cocaine. She had only ever smelled marijuana before, but it had a sweet smell, too.

A board creaked as she stepped on to the landing, but, although she froze for a second, it aroused no reaction. The landing was as silent as the rooms downstairs had been, and she felt her nails digging into her palms as she made her way to Conor's bedroom door. It wasn't completely closed, just pushed to, and with her

tongue trapped between her teeth she widened it until
her head could fit into the opening.

And then she sucked in a gulp of air. Conor was there,
sure enough, stretched out flat on the bed, with only a
sheet to cover his nakedness. But the relief she felt at
finding him was instantly forgotten when she saw the
capsules scattered over the top of the bedside unit. Some
had even spilled on to the carpet, along with the now
empty glass of water he must have used to swallow them.

Oh, lord!

The air left her lungs in a panic-stricken rush, and,
abandoning any doubts about how she came to be here,
she hurried to the bed. 'Conor,' she cried, grasping his
shoulder and shaking him urgently. 'Conor, wake up!'

His skin felt cold to the touch, and for one awful
moment she thought she was too late. Was that sweet
smell, which was so much stronger here, the smell of
death? The taste of the peanut butter sandwiches she
had eaten before leaving home rose sickeningly into her
throat. But she couldn't afford to be ill now, she chided,
as, to her relief, his flesh warmed beneath her hand. If
Conor was unconscious, he must have taken an overdose.
No one knew the strength of the drugs he was using better
than he did. It couldn't have been a mistake.

Then, just as the realisation that she should get him
off the bed and on to his feet and call an ambulance
brought a frantic return of sanity, she saw the blood on
the sheet. How she could have missed it earlier, she didn't
know. There was enough of it, for God's sake! But her
whole attention had been focused on the drugs. Now,
the staining that skirted his waist brought a wave of diz-
ziness sweeping over her, and this time she couldn't hold
back. She had identified the smell and it terrified her.
With a muffled cry, she ran for the bathroom, reaching
the toilet basin just in time.

She was still kneeling there, trying to find the strength to get to her feet again, when a hand descended on her shoulder. 'Liv?' Conor's voice said disbelievingly. 'God, Liv, what are you doing here?'

CHAPTER TWELVE

OLIVIA scrambled to her feet, unable for a moment to say anything. The shock of seeing him awake, and on his feet, was too much for her, and she could only cling to the toilet cistern, praying it wasn't just a dream.

Conor appeared real enough, though much paler than she remembered, his untidy hair and unshaven chin adding to his air of debilitation. But he had dragged a navy silk dressing-gown over his nakedness, and, had she not seen the blood on the sheet, she might have been persuaded that there was nothing wrong with him that a shower and a decent night's sleep wouldn't cure.

'Liv,' he repeated now, his confusion giving way to guarded weariness. 'How the hell did you get in?'

Olivia shook her head, and then wished she hadn't when the room revolved around her. She waited a moment for the giddiness to pass, and then moved determinedly towards the sink. 'Can—can I just rinse my face and hands?' she asked, hoping he wouldn't try to deter her. It was bad enough that he had caught her throwing up in his bathroom. She didn't think she could cope with an argument just yet.

However, Conor obediently stepped aside, and, turning her back on him, she hurriedly sluiced her face and hands, and cleaned her teeth with her finger. Then, feeling much better, she straightened and reached for a towel.

'Did—did I—that is, were you asleep?' she ventured nervously, slipping the towel back on to the rail, suddenly aware of how presumptuous she had been.

Conor's eyes were narrowed and unreadable. 'Obviously,' he said at last, stepping back so that she could precede him out of the room. 'Now, how much longer are we going to continue this, before you tell me what in hell is going on?'

Olivia drew a steadying breath, and paused on the landing, not sure which direction to take. The obvious choice was to go back into Conor's bedroom, but she no longer had the temerity to believe that she would be welcome there. So instead she turned towards the stairs.

He followed her down, and, remembering the blood she had seen on the sheet, Olivia found herself biting her lower lip. She wanted to ask what it was, what had happened, but she didn't have the nerve. She was already having to face the fact that Conor didn't want her here, any more than he had wanted anyone else. Was he going to escort her off the premises, without even giving her a chance to tell him why she'd come?

But, when they reached the lower floor, he said, 'The kitchen,' and, breathing a little more easily, Olivia walked along the hall. But she was aware of him behind her, watching her every move.

It was getting dark, she noticed, a fact that was endorsed when Conor switched on the track of spotlights. They immediately darkened the windows, and cast shadows on to his hollow cheeks, accentuating his pallor and the unforgiving twist of his lips.

'Sit down,' he said, but she preferred to stand, and with a careless shrug he hooked out a chair and dropped into it. A stab of pain crossed his face as he did so, betraying that unseen injury, but his expression warned against her offering sympathy. 'Well?' he prompted, as she pushed her anxious hands into her pockets, and leaned against one of the dark oak units. 'Go on. I'm listening.'

Olivia drew a breath. 'I did ring the bell,' she began, rather lamely. 'And—and knocked. But I couldn't make you hear.'

'How do you know?'

His question confused her, and she gazed at him uncertainly. 'How do you know what?'

'How do you know I didn't hear you?'

'Oh.' Encountering his cool, enigmatic gaze, Olivia was half prepared to accept that he had heard her after all. But she couldn't let that deter her. 'Well, I can't be sure, of course——'

'No, you can't.'

'—but you were—asleep—when I came into the bedroom.'

'Was I?'

'Oh, Conor!' Her helpless cry seemed to affect him. His cheeks drew in, and a muscle jerked with spasmodic insistence. But he obviously had no intention of making this easy for her, and she was forced to continue. 'Anyway,' she went on, 'I was—worried about you.' And, responding to his scornful expression, 'I was! After—after what...' She bit back Mrs Drake's name, and proceeded awkwardly, 'I—wanted to see you.'

'Why?'

'Why?' She lifted her shoulders as a convincing answer escaped her. 'Why do you think?'

Conor lay back in his chair, and, although she was sure he would have preferred her not to see it, he couldn't disguise the wince of pain that brought a sudden starkness to his pale features. Almost involuntarily, his hand moved to protect his midriff, and her mouth dried at the thought that he might have more than one injury. But his cold face forbade any mention of the fact, and she was forced to watch his efforts to cover his reaction in silence.

'I—think—someone—contacted you,' he said at last, and, aware of what it had cost him to speak normally, Olivia wondered how she had ever found the courage to leave him. She wanted to put her arms around him so badly that it was a physical effort not to do so, but she was so afraid that he would reject her. 'Who was it?' he went on. 'Sharon? Aunt Elizabeth?' He frowned, resting his elbow on the edge of the table, and dropping his head against his hand. 'There is no one else.'

Olivia hesitated. And then, realising they couldn't go on unless they were completely honest with one another, she said, 'It was Mrs Drake, actually,' and he groaned.

'I knew it,' he muttered. 'I knew you wouldn't have come here of your own free will!'

'That's not true!' Olivia was defensive.

'No?' Conor sounded weary now. 'Don't tell me—you were packing your bag to come down here when you got the message.'

'No. I was at Stephen's funeral, actually,' replied Olivia quietly, and this time she was sure she had his full attention.

'Say what?'

'I said——'

'Dammit, I heard what you said,' he exclaimed, lifting his head. He ran a hand that shook slightly through the unruly tangle of his hair. 'But—how? Did he have an accident?'

Olivia shrugged. 'It was a heart attack,' she said simply. 'According to his doctor, there was a weakness. It could have happened any time.'

'Shit!' Conor closed his eyes for a moment, and when he opened them again his face was paler than before. 'And I guess I contributed to the attack, didn't I? He must have guessed there was something going on between us.'

'No!' Olivia's renunciation was vehement. 'He'd been warned not to overdo things, but Stephen never would listen to anyone's advice.'

Conor blinked. 'Isn't that pretty callous? Even for you?'

Olivia noticed the qualification, but now was not the time to take him up on it. How callous she had been in leaving him only time would tell, but for now she had to concentrate on other matters.

'You don't understand,' she began, pushing herself away from the unit, but Conor wouldn't let her finish.

'Your husband's just died, for God's sake!' he muttered savagely. 'For pity's sake, Liv, you've just buried him today!'

Olivia expelled the air in her lungs in a long sigh. 'He wasn't my husband,' she said, linking her fingers together. 'Our divorce became final just after I got back to London.'

Conor came up out of his chair with a baleful oath. 'What?'

'It's true.' Olivia was nervous of the look on his face, but she had to go on. 'I—I asked Stephen for a divorce before I had the accident,' she blurted. 'He—he had been seeing other women, and when I found out...' She licked her lips. 'He didn't agree at first. But... when I was in the hospital, he—changed his mind.'

Conor was supporting himself against the edge of the table. 'But—he came here,' he said harshly. 'He spent the night at the inn. Mrs Drake told me.'

'I know.' Olivia gazed at him despairingly. 'But she could have also told you that we had separate rooms. You see, Stephen was in some trouble over—over his boss's wife, and he needed an alibi.'

A pulse was beating in Conor's temple. She could see it, hammering away under the skin. It was the only evidence she had that his reaction to what she was saying was not all negative. Surely that erratic little vibration wasn't wholly motivated by anger? Why should he react so violently if it meant nothing to him?

'So, you were lying,' he said now, and her heart sank at his words. 'God, Liv, was it so hard to tell me you didn't want to get involved?'

'It wasn't like that!' Olivia took a couple of steps towards him, and then halted uncertainly. 'Conor, you know my—marriage—wasn't a problem with us.'

'Wasn't it?' There was accusation in his eyes, and she gave an inward groan at the seeming impossibility of her task.

'No,' she insisted now. Then, unable to sustain the implacability of his gaze, she bent her head. 'Don't pretend you believed everything I said.'

Conor swore. 'I don't know what I believe any more,' he stated unevenly. 'Are you telling me you've changed your mind?'

Olivia swallowed and lifted her head. 'And if I am?'

Conor stared at her for a long, disbelieving minute, and then he swung away, making for the window, gripping the sink below it with white-knuckled hands. He looked out of the window for so long that what little confidence Olivia had had evaporated, and by the time he turned his head to look at her again she was visibly shaking.

'Why did you come here, Liv?' he asked, and, of all the things she had thought he might say, this was the least expected.

'I—I've told you,' she said, wishing she had something to hold on to. 'I wanted to see you.'

Conor's lips twisted. 'Yes. But would you have come if some do-gooding individual hadn't chosen to tell you I was a mess?'

'Yes——'

'Yes?' He didn't sound convinced. 'Liv, that little scene upstairs said more about you than you know. God knows what tale Mrs Drake had spun you, but when you came into the bedroom you thought I was unconscious!'

Olivia hesitated. 'Maybe.'

'There's no "maybe" about it,' he exclaimed, angrily. 'Because you couldn't get a reply, you thought I'd taken an overdose, didn't you? And that really scared you. So much so that you were puking up your guts when I walked into the bathroom.'

'All right.' Olivia saw no point in denying it. 'I did get a shock when I saw you. There were capsules all over the bedside cabinet, and blood on the sheet——'

'Dried blood,' he cut in sharply.

'—and I—I panicked.'

Conor turned to face her. 'There was no need. I dropped the bottle as I was taking a couple of pain-killers, that's all. If I'd known I was expecting a visitor, I'd have picked them up.'

Olivia took a breath. 'What about the blood?'

'I cut myself,' he replied dismissively.

'And the accident?'

'What accident?'

'The accident at the clinic,' she persisted. 'Mrs Drake said——'

'Mrs Drake should learn to mind her own business,' he retorted. 'I had a—a run-in with an irate visitor, that was all. It was something and nothing. Certainly not serious enough to bring you haring down from London.'

'That wasn't why...' began Olivia swiftly, and then made an impatient gesture. What was the point? He wasn't going to believe her, whatever she said.

Conor left the sink and came back to rest his palms on the table. She suspected it was because, whatever he said, he needed some support. But his next words sent all other thoughts out of her head.

'Tell me,' he said, dispassionately, 'what would you have done if I had been unconscious? I'd like to know.'

'What would I...?' Olivia gasped. 'I'd have called an ambulance, of course.'

'Would you?' He looked at her through the veil of his lashes. 'Even though it would have meant getting involved?'

Olivia caught her breath. 'What do you mean?'

'Well...' Conor straightened with an evident effort. 'You have left me before. And you didn't care then whether I lived or died.'

'My God!' Olivia was horrified. 'Of course I cared. I've always...' She bit back the shaming admission, but the look in his eyes forced her to go on. 'Do you hate me that much?'

'I don't hate you at all,' he told her succinctly, his voice breaking on the words. 'And believe me, I've tried!'

'Oh, Conor!'

Unable to hold back any longer, Olivia gave in to the sexual tension that had been building inside her. She couldn't wait to hear if he was going to reject her. If he did, then so be it, but for this moment in time she had to feel his arms about her. Moving too quickly for him to evade her, she circled the table until there was barely a hand's-breadth between them. Then, reaching up, she cupped his face in her hands, and brought his unwary mouth to hers.

He sucked in his breath as she pressed herself against him, but when she would have drawn back again his hands went swiftly to her waist, and held her where she was. 'Not now,' he breathed, against her lips, and when his tongue slid into her mouth her legs felt too weak to disobey him.

She clung to him desperately, to the solid warmth of bone and muscle she had dreamed for so long of holding. His heart was thudding against his ribs, his skin smooth and male beneath her hands. He was impatient and ungentle, but so familiar, and she felt her senses swimming beneath his urgent assault.

He kissed her many times—hard, angry kisses at first, which gradually gave way to the sensuality of passion. He wanted to hurt her, as she had hurt him, but he seemed to realise as his kisses gentled that he was only hurting himself.

'I should kill you for what you've done to me,' he muttered, when his lips sought the scented curve of her neck. His fingers stroked the vulnerable skin and tightened perceptibly. 'Do you know you nearly killed me when you walked out like that?'

'I have some idea,' she confessed unsteadily. 'I haven't exactly found it easy myself. I'm still not sure it's the best thing for both of us. But when I heard about the accident I couldn't keep away.'

He drew back briefly to look down at her. 'You'd better be sure now,' he said roughly, cupping her face in his hand. 'Because, whatever it takes, I'm not going to let you go this time.'

'I—don't want you to,' she assured him huskily, turning her lips against his fingers. 'That's what I came to tell you. Only, as usual, I made a mess of it.'

Conor's lips twisted. 'Am I supposed to believe that?'

'Yes.' Olivia's response was defensive at first, but then, glimpsing the mockery in his eyes, she grabbed his arms and shook him. 'It's not funny,' she said fiercely. 'I love you, you big idiot!'

Conor's response was to utter a muffled moan and slump heavily against her. His weight pinned her against the fridge-freezer behind her, and for a moment she thought he was still teasing. But his eyes were closed, and there was a thin film of sweat on his forehead, and when she tried to push him away from her he didn't resist.

'Conor!' she exclaimed, horror-stricken, convinced he had now passed out. But, as her brain struggled to cope with this disaster, he put a hand on the unit and pushed himself away from her: weaker, paler, but unmistakably alert.

'Sorry about that,' he muttered ruefully, groping for the table behind him, and sinking down on to its rim. 'I guess the relief was just too much for me. It won't happen again.'

'No, it won't,' said Olivia, more forcefully than she felt. She wasn't deceived by his attempt to dismiss what had happened as relief. Propelling herself towards him, she took advantage of his weakness to part the lapels of his dressing-gown, catching her breath, aghast, at the ugly gash that scarred his midriff.

'Hey, do you mind?' he protested mildly, as the gown threatened to open completely. 'I don't mind you seeing me naked, but not in front of the neighbours, please!'

But Olivia wasn't listening to this attempt to distract her. She was gazing at the wound, which her playfulness had caused to weep a little, and she felt like weeping herself for the pain she must have caused him.

'This is why they were so concerned about you at the clinic, isn't it?' she exclaimed, gazing at him with worried eyes. 'Oh, Conor—love—why haven't you had it properly attended to? You're a doc——'

'Say that again,' broke in Conor irrepressibly, catching her wrists, and pulling her between his legs. 'That bit where you called me "love". I like it.'

But Olivia wouldn't let him get away with it, even though she couldn't prevent herself from responding to the tender kiss he bestowed at the corner of her mouth. 'You know how easily infection can set in,' she persisted, touching the bruised flesh around the gash with delicate fingers. 'Have you had any antibiotics?'

'I'll be OK,' Conor told her gently. 'Now that you're here, I'll do anything you want.' His thumbs brushed the sensitive inner curve of her wrists, before he bent to kiss them. 'I didn't much care what happened to me before.'

'Oh, Conor,' she exclaimed, smoothing back the hair from his damp forehead with a shaking hand. 'If only I'd known.'

'I thought you did know,' he replied gravely. 'What do you think I meant when I told you I loved you?'

Olivia couldn't allow herself to think of that now. 'How—how did it happen?' she asked instead, releasing herself from Conor's grasp, and moving to the sink. 'You said something about a visitor,' she added, concentrating on turning on the taps. 'Um—do you still keep the first-aid box in this top cupboard?'

Conor sighed, but he nodded, and, standing on tiptoe, Olivia brought down the small first-aid chest, which had been kept in that cupboard when Conor was a baby. 'Always keep medicines out of the reach of children,' Sally had used to say, and Olivia remembered feeling very grown-up because Sally had let her get the box down.

She didn't feel grown-up now. She felt ignorant and inexperienced, and totally incapable of dealing with such a dangerous-looking injury. She was sure he needed hospital treatment, but he was unlikely to agree to that. So she would have to think positively, and do the best she could.

Sorting through the plastic tapes and bandages, she soon realised that most, if not all of these things had been in the box since Sally's day. A bottle of camomile lotion, which she had once used to cool Conor's spots when he had chicken-pox, was crusted and sedimentary, and the tubes of antiseptic had all split with age. She wouldn't have used the iodine she found to corrode metal, let alone to treat human tissue. Even the surgical scissors were rusting in their case.

'This is useless!' she exclaimed, lifting her head and looking at him, and she realised he had only let her waste her time because it had given him room to recover.

'Stop fussing,' he said, his eyes dark and disturbing. 'I'll survive. Now, why don't we go upstairs and finish what we started?'

Olivia sighed. 'Conor——'

'All right, all right. I'll put some alcohol on it,' he exclaimed, pushing himself up from the table, and swaying on his feet. 'If you look in that drawer, you'll find some new plasters. That's all I've been using, and it's worked so far.'

'Has it?' Olivia gave him a dubious glance, before crossing the room and opening the drawer he had indicated. She came back to where he was standing, and pushing him back on to the table. 'Now, are you going to tell me what happened?'

Conor scowled. 'If I must.'

'You must,' she assured him unsteadily, drawing the sides of his robe apart again to reveal the purpling flesh. 'Um...' She swallowed. 'Where—where do you keep the alcohol? Oh—I remember. In the drawing-room, isn't it?'

'There's a bottle of scotch in that cupboard behind you,' Conor conceded, but as she would have turned to

get it he grasped her hand. 'You don't have to do this,
you know. I can do it myself.'

'I—I want to,' she said, and Conor muttered an oath
as he briefly pulled her into his arms.

'But afterwards,' he told her hoarsely, and there was
no question what he promised...

An hour later, Olivia was sitting, cross-legged, on the
bed in the spare room, watching Conor as he slept.
Asleep, he looked so young and vulnerable, and her heart
ached at all the time she'd wasted. Life wasn't about
certainties, she thought, with the insight that being in
love had brought her. At best, it could only be an im-
ponderable. There was no way she could be sure that
Conor wouldn't hurt her, but because they loved each
other they had a better chance than most.

And she could so easily have lost everything, she
thought shakily, unable to prevent herself from stroking
the silky hair that shadowed his rib-cage. The man Conor
had surprised, selling cocaine to one of his patients in
the men's lavatories at the clinic, could so easily have
destroyed their future. As it was, the knife had he drawn
had gouged an ugly furrow in Conor's midriff, before
Conor had dashed it from his grasp. Even then, it was
only the fact that one of the other doctors had come
into the men's room that had stopped him from finishing the job. Conor had been losing blood rapidly, and
it was arguable how long he could have held out against
such a desperate assailant.

Not that Conor had said as much. On the contrary,
he had insisted on making light of it, even when the alcohol Olivia had used to cleanse the wound must have
been tearing him apart. It had taken all her will and
determination to dress the wound afterwards, but she
had known she had to do it. And Conor had assured
her it wasn't life-threatening.

Nevertheless, she intended to make sure he looked after
himself from now on. There was no way she was going

to risk losing what she had found. The future, which had once seemed so bleak, was now full of promise. The day that had started so badly had ended so well.

'What are you thinking about?'

Conor's drowsy voice interrupted her reverie, and, for the first time, she didn't rush to cover herself when he looked at her. In the lamplight, her pale skin had a pearly lustre, and Conor was not immune to the nearness of her flesh.

Pushing himself up on his elbows, he regarded her with evident satisfaction, brushing the tumbling darkness of her hair aside, and trailing one finger from her throat to the rosy tip of her breast. Her breasts were still tingling from the eager attention of his mouth, and they responded to his caresses with a totally shameless ease.

'Mmm—come here,' he said, and beneath the thin sheet that covered him from the waist she could see the unmistakable hardening of his arousal. It was still a source of amazement—and delight—to her that she could do this to him, and, although she was tempted to give in to him again, there were things she had to say.

'Not yet,' she murmured, slipping off the bed and wrapping his discarded dressing-gown about her. 'We— we have to talk.'

'Why?' Conor's eyes were wary now, and, had she been more sure of herself, she'd have recognised his anxiety. As it was, she was still troubled by her own sense of inadequacy, and she had no idea how he would react to the things she had to tell him.

'Because we do,' she replied now, lifting her hands to free her hair from the collar of the dressing-gown. As she did so, the robe parted again, and she hurriedly gathered it together, over the swelling mound of her stomach.

Conor didn't notice. He was too intent on her words, and, pushing himself up against the pillows, he linked his hands behind his head. 'All right,' he said, completely unaware of the provocation of the growth of golden hair in his armpits. It was ridiculous, she thought, but there was something so sensual about Conor's body hair. It made her want to go to him, and bury her face in the musky smell of him, and, in spite of her determined practicality, it showed.

And Conor recognised it at once. His own anxiety melted beneath the yearning look in her eyes, and, throwing back the covers, he went after her.

She turned away from his too-appealing beauty, but all he did was slide his arms around her waist from behind, drawing her back against him. 'Be careful,' she said, ever conscious of the dressing on his midriff, but he only made a dismissing sound and buried his face in the hollow of her neck.

'Come back to bed,' he said. 'We can talk there.' His hands parted the robe and slid inside, over the throbbing fullness of her breasts. 'You know you want to. And we can talk in the morning.'

Olivia drew a trembling breath, and for a moment she gave in and yielded against him. But then the importance of what she had to tell him forced her to stiffen, and Conor said an oath, and turned her round to face him.

'OK,' he said. 'What is it? You're not going to tell me this isn't real, I hope?' His face was strained, and she suddenly realised what he was afraid of. In spite of all she had said, he still had doubts about her motives for being here.

Shaking her head, she lifted her hands to his face. 'I love you,' she said. 'I guess I've always loved you. But I was afraid to tell you. I was afraid of being hurt.'

Conor's smile was rueful. 'So you hurt me instead.'

'I hurt us both,' she admitted huskily. 'You see, I was sure that what you felt for me was just infatuation. That if I went away you'd realise that truth.'

'Oh, Liv!' He grasped one of her hands and brought it to his mouth. 'You should have known it wasn't infatuation. God,' he groaned, 'I'd been crazy about you since I was a teenager. Only you always seemed so—remote, after you went to live in London. Then, when Mum and Dad died, it was like a living hell for a while. I'd lost everything I loved—everyone I loved, including you. No.' His smile was gentle. 'Most especially you. No wonder I went to pieces. That's why I owe Aunt Elizabeth so much. She and Uncle Philip stuck with me, even when I let them down.'

Olivia frowned. 'What do you mean?'

'I mean, I got involved in the drug scene myself,' said Conor heavily. 'Oh, not cocaine or heroin. But I smoked pot, and that day I got up the courage to come see you in London I was really high. The first and last time I used drugs to give me confidence,' he added grimly. 'I knew I'd blown any chance of making it with you after that, and, believe me, that was a powerful deterrent.'

'Oh, love!'

She reached up to kiss him, and for a few moments there was silence in the room. But then, reluctantly, he lifted his head.

'Anyway,' he went on slowly, 'I kicked the habit after that. I worked hard, and I graduated from med. school, and then I told Aunt Elizabeth that I wanted to come and work in London. I knew I wanted to see you again, and I guess I was hoping it still might work out. But,' he shrugged, 'when I checked out your old address, the landlady there told me you'd left to get married.' He shook his head. 'That was a pretty bad day.'

Olivia was amazed. 'I never knew.'

'No. How could you? I didn't have the guts to come and say hi. Not when I knew how much I was hurting. I didn't want to hear how happy you were with somebody else.'

Olivia sighed. 'So—you came back here?'

'Eventually.' He grimaced. 'It dawned on me that you might have children by now, and I didn't want to know about them either. Then when you turned up, practically on my doorstep, I couldn't believe it. God, it was like a sign. I thought, somebody up there likes me after all.'

Olivia grimaced. 'I was so embarrassed that morning.'

'I wasn't. I was on cloud nine.' He grinned. 'Until I met Stephen, that is. Then, all I wanted to do was break his neck.'

'Poor Stephen.'

'Yes, poor Stephen.' Conor acknowledged the truth of her words. 'This must have been quite a day for you. And then driving down here tonight.'

Olivia's lips twitched. 'I wanted to.'

'Yes.' Conor bent to kiss her. 'I'm so glad you did.' He frowned. 'But that reminds me, how did you get in?'

'Through the cellar,' she admitted ruefully. 'I'm afraid I broke the padlock. Will you forgive me?'

'I'll forgive you anything,' he told her huskily. 'After these weeks of going around like a zombie, all I want to do is show you how much I love you, and marry you as soon as possible. Now, is that clear enough for you, or would you like it in writing?'

Olivia shook her head. 'And if I were to tell you...'

She broke off, her courage giving out on her at the last minute, and Conor scowled. 'If you were to tell me what?' he demanded. 'Liv, for pity's sake. What is it now?'

For an answer, she took his hand and brought it to the slight mound of her stomach. 'I'm—pregnant,' she said, watching anxiously for his reaction, and Conor's jaw sagged as he felt the unmistakable swelling.

'Pregnant?' he said, in a shaken voice. 'But you said— you and Stephen——'

Olivia gasped. 'Conor!' she exclaimed. 'This has nothing to do with Stephen! I—it's yours! I mean—ours! Yours and mine.'

Conor blinked. 'But I thought——'

'I know what you thought. I'd said that Stephen and I had never had a child. And we haven't. But it just obviously wasn't meant to be. Whereas this——'

Conor swallowed. 'So when you said you'd been thinking of coming to see me, this—this was why?'

Olivia felt a momentary chill, but she nodded.

Conor absorbed this for a moment, and then he said flatly, 'How long have you know about it?'

Olivia lifted her shoulders. 'A month, six weeks.' She gazed helplessly at him. 'Why? Aren't you—aren't you pleased?'

Conor turned away from her. 'Whether I'm pleased or not doesn't have a lot to do with it, does it?' he muttered, raking back his hair in that gesture she was coming to know so well. 'My God! So that's why you're prepared to marry me now. To get a name for your baby.'

'Conor!' Olivia stared at his back disbelievingly, and for a sickening moment she felt as if everything she had had had been torn away from her. She had been afraid it might happen, of course. That was one of the reasons why she had been so nervous about telling him in the first place.

But he was like her, she realised suddenly, as the force of her convictions gave her back her strength. He was so afraid now of being hurt, and it was up to her to prove to him that those desperate days were over.

'I—could get an abortion, if that's what you want,' she offered softly, as he riffled in his wardrobe and pulled on a pair of drawstring trousers, and he turned to her incredulously.

'What did you say?'

'I said—it's not too late for me to have an abortion,' she replied evenly, playing with the cord of his robe. 'Well,' she added, as his face contorted with emotion, 'if that's what it takes to make you believe I love you, and not what you can give me, so be it.' She took a step towards him, and then finished breathlessly, 'I don't care any more if we never have a baby. It's you I want, Conor. Do I have to put it in writing, too?'

He didn't hesitate then. His need for her was too great, and with a groan of anguish he pulled her into his arms.

'Do you mean it?' he choked, cupping her face in his hands and staring down at her as if he'd read the answer in her soul. 'You want me with or without this baby?'

'How can you doubt it?' she whispered brokenly. 'I never want us to be parted again.'

Conor stared at her. 'You mean it.'

'You'd better believe it,' she assured him unsteadily, hardly able to believe herself that everything was going to be all right. 'Darling, you have a very poor opinion of me if you think I'd risk another disastrous marriage, just to give your child a name. That's why I was afraid to come and tell you. I didn't want you to marry me just because you felt responsible.'

'Oh, Liv, how could you think that?'

'You did,' she reminded him softly. 'Which reminds me, you haven't told me how you feel.'

'Me?' Conor was bemused. 'It seems like a dream.' He shook his head. 'If you're happy, I'm happy.' And then, 'But do you mind? About giving up your work, I mean?'

'I'm—ecstatic,' she told him honestly. 'As far as my work is concerned, I think I deserve a break. About five years' break, at least,' she dimpled becomingly. 'Or longer, depending on the size of our family.'

'Liv——'

'But now I think we should get some sleep,' she said firmly. 'It's going to be morning soon. And you need some rest.'

Conor grinned. 'Oh, it's a long time until morning,' he assured her huskily. 'But I like the way you said *we* should get some sleep. At last I've got you where you belong: in my bed!'

Share the adventure—and the romance—of

HARLEQUIN PRESENTS®

A Year
DOWN UNDER

If you missed any titles in this miniseries,
here's your chance to order them:

Harlequin Presents®—A Year Down Under

#11519	HEART OF THE OUTBACK by Emma Darcy	$2.39	☐
#11527	NO GENTLE SEDUCTION by Helen Bianchin	$2.89	☐
#11537	THE GOLDEN MASK by Robyn Donald	$2.89	☐
#11546	A DANGEROUS LOVER by Lindsay Armstrong	$2.89	☐
#11554	SECRET ADMIRER by Susan Napier	$2.89	☐
#11562	OUTBACK MAN by Miranda Lee	$2.99	☐
#11570	NO RISKS, NO PRIZES by Emma Darcy	$2.99	☐
#11577	THE STONE PRINCESS by Robyn Donald	$2.99	☐
#11586	AND THEN CAME MORNING by Daphne Clair	$2.99	☐
#11595	WINTER OF DREAMS by Susan Napier	$2.99	☐
#11601	RELUCTANT CAPTIVE by Helen Bianchin	$2.99	☐
#11611	SUCH DARK MAGIC by Robyn Donald	$2.99	☐

(limited quantities available on certain titles)

TOTAL AMOUNT	$
POSTAGE & HANDLING	$
($1.00 for one book, 50¢ for each additional)	
APPLICABLE TAXES*	$ _____
TOTAL PAYABLE	$ _____

(check or money order—please do not send cash)

To order, complete this form and send it, along with a check or money order for the total above, payable to Harlequin Books, to: *In the U.S.*: 3010 Walden Avenue, P.O. Box 9047, Buffalo, NY 14269-9047; *In Canada*: P.O. Box 613, Fort Erie, Ontario, L2A 5X3.

Name: _____

Address: _____ City: _____

State/Prov.: _____ Zip/Postal Code: _____

*New York residents remit applicable sales taxes.
Canadian residents remit applicable GST and provincial taxes.　　　　YDUF

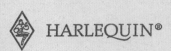 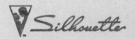

POSTCARDS FROM EUROPE
HARLEQUIN PRESENTS®

Travel across Europe in 1994 with
Harlequin Presents. Collect a new
Postcards From Europe title each month!

Don't miss
MASK OF DECEPTION
by Sara Wood
Harlequin Presents #1628

*Available in February wherever
Harlequin Presents books are sold.*

HPPFE2

Hi—
*It's carnival time in
Italy! The streets of
Venice are filled
with music—the
costumes are
incredible. And
I can't wait to
tell you about
Lucenzo Salviati...
Love, Meredith*

Are you looking for more titles by

ANNE MATHER

Don't miss these fabulous stories by one of
Harlequin's most distinguished authors:

Harlequin Presents®

#11354	INDISCRETION	$2.75	☐
#11444	BLIND PASSION	$2.89	☐
#11458	SUCH SWEET POISON	$2.89	☐
#11492	BETRAYED	$2.89	☐
#11542	GUILTY	$2.89	☐
#11567	RICH AS SIN	$2.99	☐
#11591	TIDEWATER SEDUCTION	$2.99	☐

(limited quantities available on certain titles)

TOTAL AMOUNT	$
POSTAGE & HANDLING	$
($1.00 for one book, 50¢ for each additional)	
APPLICABLE TAXES*	$_____
TOTAL PAYABLE	$_____
(check or money order—please do not send cash)	

To order, complete this form and send it, along with a check or money order for the
total above, payable to Harlequin Books, to: *In the U.S.:* 3010 Walden Avenue,
P.O. Box 9047, Buffalo, NY 14269-9047; *In Canada:* P.O. Box 613, Fort Erie, Ontario,
L2A 5X3.

Name: _____

Address: _____ City: _____

State/Prov.: _____ Zip/Postal Code: _____

*New York residents remit applicable sales taxes.
 Canadian residents remit applicable GST and provincial taxes.

HAMBACK1

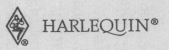 HARLEQUIN®